MISFIT

ALETHEA FAUST

For the misfits.

AUTHOR'S NOTE

This fantasy romance novella takes place in the same world as the Sex Wizards series. However, you do not need to read the main series to read and enjoy *Misfit*, though reading *Starshine* before starting this novella is recommended.

Please note that the magic in this world is derived from various sexual acts, and such acts are written in detail in this novella. Included in these scenes are: an inherent power imbalance between a Grandmaster and a new adept, bondage, dominance, submission, emotionally pointed degradation, physical overpowering, orgasm control, mentions of cuckholding, and sex with multiple partners.

Other potentially triggering content includes: violence, mentions of death and murder, brief drug use, mentions of past alcohol abuse, memories and discussions of sexual violence and rape, and classism.

I

Arlon was no stranger to feeling out of place, but standing in front of the entire population of the Crux made him want to sink into the fucking floor.

"I'm pleased to formally introduce you all to Arlon Kalisson." The Grandmaster's voice carried across the silent room, and if she hadn't been standing right beside him, he might have walked off.

"You likely will recognize him," Fawn continued. "Arlon was previously a member of our staff, but after displaying magical aptitude, he will now be joining our ranks as a wizard of the Crux."

Calling him one of the staff was a kind lie, but some of the wizards in the crowd before him knew the truth. A little over a year ago, they'd been at Fawn's side when she arrested him. In the ripple of murmurs, Arlon already felt the rumor mill starting to churn.

"Regardless of his nontraditional start at the Crux, I expect everyone to extend him the same welcome and respect you would give every new adept that comes through our doors." Her voice carried an edge that cut through the chatter.

Yet nothing Fawn said could erase who he had been. For a moment, Arlon saw himself as the wizards in front of him did; his towering height, his intimidating build. Every scar crossing his swarthy skin made him stick out among these soft and beautiful highborns like a thorn. A Wolf in wizard's robes.

Fawn's announcements turned to other things, new assignments, an update about one of the hard points in the abjuration tower, and Arlon took that as permission to step away from the front of the room. Eyes still followed him, but that wasn't unusual. His size had always caught stares, but there was something behind the looks of the Crux wizards that made him uneasy. Like they were trying to figure out where to put a blade to drop him.

He passed the gawking wizards without making eye contact, intent on the breakfast spread across the far table. Yet as he filled two cups, one with kaffa and the other with tea, he couldn't help but overhear some whispers.

"He was really a bandit?"

"Heard he was part of Vian's Wolves, up in the Hobokins."

"Gods, he's built like a brick house."

"Think he's ever killed someone?"

Arlon's hands tightened around the mugs, and he left the mess hall without grabbing anything else. He walked the familiar path across the atrium and headed down the hall towards the Grandmaster's office. The door was unlocked, and though the room belonged to Fawn, it was the one place in the Crux that didn't make him feel like a stray sneaking into a rubbage pile. Like he was intruding someplace he shouldn't be.

Arlon closed the door behind him, glad to shut the rest of the Crux away. A few moments later, Fawn entered, carrying two bowls of the breakfast he had failed to gather. He wordlessly traded her for the cup of tea he'd brought, sighing as he looked down at the spiced oats topped with spring berries.

"That was painful," Arlon murmured as Fawn circled him to take a seat behind her desk.

"That was necessary." Eyes as calm and blue as a glacial lake studied his face. "You've been a free man for two months, Arlon. People have noticed you, but you haven't so much as introduced yourself to the rest of the Crux."

He set the bowl down, his appetite suddenly gone, and picked up his kaffa instead. He'd been in such a hurry to leave the mess hall that he hadn't added anything to it, but the bitterness suited his mood this morning.

Fawn read his silence as she brushed a wayward strand of black hair over the short knifepoint of her ear. "Arlon, do you really want to make magic?"

"Of course I do, I just..."

"Just what?"

He answered with a half shrug before he took another sip of kaffa. It was hot enough to burn his tongue, but the discomfort was easier to bear than Fawn's scrutiny.

"To make magic, you have to at least *talk* to other wizards," she pressed gently.

"I talk to you, don't I?"

"You know what I mean." Fawn always seemed to have an inherent smile on her lips, which made the frown she directed at him now seem even more out of place. He didn't like seeing it, let alone being the cause of it, so he chose to look at the dark kaffa in his mug rather than her.

"What's stopping you?" she asked at last.

Silence had always been her greatest weapon, and she used it now, letting the quiet stretch until Arlon squirmed. He sunk down petulantly into the chair before he finally spoke. "I don't like the way they look at me."

Fawn considered him before she set her mug on the desk and rose to her feet. Her silver dress swept along the floor as she circled around and came to stand behind his chair. Her long-fingered hands rested on his shoulders, squeezing gently. "Why?"

Arlon gave another half shrug, but over the past two months, her touch had become a conditioned thing, easing the tension from his body. It was as if her calming presence seeped into him through the simple contact. It took a moment for him to find the answer, but even before she'd granted him his freedom, she had given him the tools to better sort through his own emotions.

"I was indentured two months ago," he said. "Just because you've given me robes doesn't change the fact that I started here in chains."

"Aah," Fawn said in that knowing way that used to grate on him like dirt in a wound. "You think they're judging you. Judging your past." He gave another little half shrug only to groan as her thumb dug into a knot in the muscles of his shoulder. "But if you refuse to speak to anyone, what else have you given them to consider? Certainly not the man you are now."

He scowled at that. "Ah, yes. Let me, one of Vian's Wolves, scourge of the Hobokins, waltz up to these nobles and highborns to broach a conversation."

"Former scourge of the Hobokins," Fawn corrected with a delicate chuckle. She circled around to the front of his chair, bundling her silver skirts before she straddled his lap in one smooth movement. As her weight settled against him, his hands automatically came up to rest on the curve of her waist.

"Calling all who live in the Crux nobles and highborns is very generalizing. Also incorrect."

"Oh?" Arlon asked, eyebrow raised. "I thought you said wizards like me were rare."

"And they are," Fawn said. "But regardless, you aren't the only non-bloodline wizard currently in residence. Two others have been here for some time, now. They arrived a few months before your indenture even started."

A frown tugged at his lips as he wracked his memory for anyone at breakfast who stood out. "Really? Who?"

"I wager you would find out if you asked around." Mischief lit up her blue eyes, and she stole his frown away with a gentle kiss.

Arlon let out an annoyed sigh against her lips even as his eyes slid closed. The annoyance faded as the kiss deepened, and when she finally pulled away, his trousers were uncomfortably tight.

"Why can't I just make magic with you?" he asked, fully aware of how pathetic the longing in his voice sounded.

Funny how things had changed. When Fawn had arrested him over a year ago, he had thought he hated her. Now, cut loose among the greater population of the Crux, he felt lost without her.

During the year he had served his sentence, Fawn had shown him all the miracles magic could accomplish. He'd gotten glimpses, but it wasn't until the night he gained his freedom that she showed him *exactly* how it was made. The past two months had been eye-opening, and though he knew that embracing the magic in his blood could change the course of his life for the better, he didn't know where to start.

Fawn's smile was full of sympathy as she lifted her hands to cup his face. Her long, cool fingers lacked the extra joint that full-blooded Maeve had, but he couldn't imagine a safer place to be than in between them.

"*A'marra*, I will never force you to cast or conduit for anyone else if that's what you choose," she said gently. "What I'm asking you to do is find *friendship*." Before his scowl could fully form, Fawn kissed it away. "I know trust is difficult for you. I understand all of the many reasons why that is. All I'm asking is that you try."

Her hands released his face, and Arlon sighed as he rubbed his cheek. She let him sit with that for a moment, let the silence stretch once more until finally, he said, "Alright. I'll find these non-bloodline wizards. Tomorrow, maybe."

A smile graced her lips as she stroked her fingers through his thick, coal-black hair. "And what were you planning on doing today?"

Arlon raised an eyebrow as his hands tightened on her hips. He pulled her flush against him, letting her feel his need through the fabric of his trousers. "If the Grandmaster can find time in her busy schedule to indulge me... I think I have a spell I'd like to try."

Fawn hummed, something mischievous entering her smile. "So you've been reading the book I loaned you?"

Heat creeped up his neck. He had expected a book called *Fundamentals of Magic* to be a dry read. He had been mistaken.

"It has been... enlightening."

Fawn ground her hips down, and Arlon groaned at the heat of her, just out of reach through so many layers of clothing. "Which schools have piqued your interest?"

"Most of them have in some way or another."

Fawn hummed again before she leaned forward, lips brushing his ear. "Is there a school in particular you would like to explore with your willing conduit today?"

The whisper of her lips against his skin sent gooseflesh down Arlon's arms. "I have some ideas."

Fawn moved off his lap, standing with one smooth motion before she offered him a hand. "Show me."

2

The dungeon, in spite of its name, was a comfortable place for Arlon. It was private and quiet, secluded from the rest of the Crux by design. He'd spent hours down here building various restraints and tools at Fawn's request, but until the night his indenture ended, he'd never used it as anything more than a workspace.

Now, surrounded by the tools of the magical trade, it suddenly became an overwhelming task to pick the right ones. In the past two months of freedom, Fawn had helped him explore the various schools on a surface level, but this was his first real attempt at crafting a spell. The many ideas he'd been carrying all scattered like a flock of birds, and faced with a full arsenal of equipment, he wasn't even sure what school to settle on.

Fawn watched him from where she was reclined on the large bed at the end of the room. The mirrors surrounding it reflected her sly grin at him three times over.

"What school have you chosen, a*'marra?*" she asked at last.

"Abjuration?"

Fawn raised one eyebrow. "Is that a question?"

"Abjuration," Arlon said again, definitively this time.

"Ropes are in the cabinet," she said, and Arlon hurried over to grab a soft hemp coil. A cloth blindfold caught his attention, and he grabbed it as well.

"Abjuration and illusion," he corrected before he moved to meet Fawn on the bed.

"His first real spell, and he's mixing schools," Fawn said approvingly. "Already an innovative spellcrafter."

"I just know what I want to do with you," he said as he knelt over her, snapping the rope taut between his hands.

Fawn's eyes smoldered as she looked up at him. "Show me."

Arlon descended, crashing his lips against hers, the ropes momentarily forgotten. He kissed her like he was starving and she was the only thing that could slake his hunger. Yet instead of satisfying him, it only left him craving more. One knee slid between her legs, and the heat of her cunt reached him even through their combined layers.

"How much do you care about this dress?" he asked, breathless in the aftermath of the kiss.

Fawn's laugh warmed him from the inside out. "I would prefer if you didn't destroy it."

"Shame," he said before he started to loosen the silk tie that laced up the front of it. "I would love to tear something off of you someday."

"That is a fantasy I'll be happy to indulge with a different dress," she said, only to gasp as Arlon pulled the front open. It exposed her collar and breasts, her skin as pale as moonlight, a trait fitting for the lunariel Maeve that made up half of her parentage.

"Gods, you're beautiful," he murmured as he shimmied her dress the rest of the way off. The last thing to go was her small clothes, pulled down her smooth legs and tossed aside to expose her fully.

She hummed as she looked up at him, her hands lifting to tease at the collar of his shirt. "Flattery can get you far with enchantment, but that's not one of the schools you picked, is it?"

"Suppose it isn't." He grabbed her slender wrists in one of his hands before pinning them over her head. "Who says this needs to be casting practice?"

Fawn hooked one leg around his waist, rocking up to grind against the bulge in his trousers. "I do."

He bit back a moan as he looked down at her in awe. Until the night he'd earned his freedom, he'd only ever seen the Grandmaster. She had been his jailer and keeper, as beautiful as she was untouchable. He still had so many things to learn about this side of her, but after pining for *months*, he was an eager student. And having permission to touch her now made it all the sweeter.

"Yes, ma'am."

She loosened her leg from around his waist and said, "You've already proven that you know how to fuck, *a'marra*. Now show me you can make magic."

"Yes, ma'am," he said again before he released her wrists and dutifully picked up the forgotten coil of rope. He was careful, making sure the ropes laid flat as he did a simple double-column tie around her wrists.

"Beautifully done," she said, only to gasp as Arlon used the tail of the rope to lift her bound wrists over her head. He tied them to one of the hard points on the headboard before he teased his fingers down her exposed sides.

"Maybe I'll bind your legs open too," he said, and he knelt between them, using his knees to push hers apart.

"You are the caster here," she reminded him, though he shivered to hear the tremble of anticipation in her voice.

Yet something about the way she said it made him pause. He was no stranger to sex. He'd had trysts among Vian's Wolves, as brief and unwise as they had been. Getting close to anyone meant giving them an opportunity to stab you in the back, so something about Fawn's trust, about being in command while she was so helpless, sent a thrill straight through him.

He'd had so little say throughout his life, so being given control here felt... sacred.

Gratitude flooded him as he knelt over her, lips brushing her chest reverently before his tongue gently lapped at one pink nipple. He savored her, enjoying her helpless squirming as he lavished the attention on her breasts, sucking her nipples to swollen points. They'd darkened from pink to red by the time he was satisfied, and only then did he kiss his way down her navel.

"Aren't you forgetting something?" Fawn asked.

For a moment, he couldn't imagine what she was talking about. When it finally hit him, he felt a little foolish.

He'd spent the better part of his indenture making focuses at Fawn's request, so how he'd forgotten them now was beyond him. He scowled, and it took all of his discipline to pull away from her and go fetch a string of uncharged focuses from the cabinet. Then, he grabbed a bottle of lube and two more coils of rope, making damn sure he was prepared so he wouldn't have to stop again.

When he returned, he made quick work of tying Fawn's ankles to the corners of the bed, leaving her just enough slack to squirm, but not enough to close herself off. For a moment, he just savored the sight, his hands stroking over her quivering thighs. Never in his twenty-six years of life did he imagine he'd have a woman like Fawn bared and trembling underneath him, yet here she was, like a dream made real. He owed her more than he could ever repay, but he was determined to try.

He slid down between her legs and was grateful he had left enough slack in the ropes to lift her hips just so. Almost like he had planned it, which he definitely hadn't. But it allowed him to close his mouth over her cunt, and he took full advantage of the happy accident.

Fawn rewarded him with a moan, her thighs straining as she found the limits of his ropes. He savored her, taking his time to run his tongue through every fold, tracing the shape of her. Carefully, he eased a finger into her wet passage as he lapped at her clit.

"F-focuses, Arlon," she reminded him. Reluctantly, he pulled away before grabbing the string of magiline beads. He prepared them with lube before he coaxed one leg open further and eased the marble against her hole. He kissed her thigh as she opened around the pearly stone before the second followed, then the third, and as he eased the last one into her, a moan broke past her full lips.

"Now may I continue?" he asked as he rubbed his fingers up the length of her dripping cunt.

"You are the caster here," she said, breathless with pleasure.

A thrill of excitement rushed through him at the reminder, and Arlon chuckled before he grabbed the blindfold and tied it over her blue eyes. As much as he trusted Fawn, it was a relief to take her gaze off of him. There was something freeing in not being watched, especially as he stripped his clothes off to join her.

And now that the requirements for the abjuration and

illusion spell had been satisfied, he proceeded to satisfy her every other way. He brought her to completion on his tongue, his fingers, savoring every shout of pleasure. She writhed under him, helpless and beautiful, and knowing that *he* was the cause of those sounds made his head swim.

It wasn't until Fawn's wrists and ankles were chafed from the ropes, her pale skin glowing with a sheen of sweat, that Arlon finally broke. He settled between her legs, arms braced over her, before he sank his aching length into her. She threw her head back with a shout of bliss, her heat contracting around him.

Energy crackled between them, wringing a moan from Arlon's pursed lips. He moved slow, savoring every inch of her as he reached down to rub her swollen clit with firm, circular strokes. He thrust deep, grinding intentionally until he brought another peak crashing through her.

Fawn's back arched, mouth open in a silent scream. The sight nearly brought his own end coursing out of him, but Arlon staved it off, barely. Instead, he reached down and pulled the string of focuses from her.

Fawn's body shuddered as each bead was freed, her cunt rippling around him as he prolonged her pleasure. He managed one last thrust before he couldn't hold back anymore. A swear broke past his lips as his own end hit. He sank deep as he emptied into her, the string of now-glowing focuses looped around his finger.

For a long moment, he didn't move, just savoring the closeness. Being with Fawn felt safe, and he was reluctant to pull away from it just yet. But eventually he did, earning a quiet sound of pleasure as he eased out of her.

"Gods," Fawn panted. She was limp under him, boneless with contentment, yet even after he untied the ropes, she remained that way. He moved onto the bed beside her, his hands gently rubbing the marks left behind. She looked up at him through heavily lidded eyes, her black hair mussed around her head. Her smile was brighter than the sun. "You are going to be a hell of a wizard someday."

Heat creeped up his neck, but he stayed quiet. Fawn had never lied to him, yet this was a hard truth to accept.

The Crux was no place for a Wolf.

3

Vian had very few rules for his Wolves, but they'd been beaten into Arlon over the years.

Rule number one, you protected the pack, and the pack would protect you. Anyone outside of the pack wasn't your friend or your family and never would be. Rule number two, don't ask questions. Vian handled the logistics, all you had to do was obey. And rule number three, you kept your fucking mouth shut. Talk to people outside of the pack only when you had to.

Arlon had broken that first rule when he helped Fawn kill the evil fucker, yet somehow, breaking the last two rules was far more difficult. But he'd promised Fawn he'd seek out the two non-bloodline wizards, and the only way to do that was to ask around.

He hated every second of it.

Approaching the beautiful highborns of the Crux was so awkward it felt downright painful. Doing it invited attention, and every time someone's eyes widened as he walked towards them, he wanted to vanish. But he did it anyway, and to his surprise, people seemed... happy to talk to him.

"Oh, you're looking for Garrett and Bridgette."

Arlon looked down at the curvy Kenitkan woman, trying to decide if that was disappointment he'd caught in her tone.

"You know them?"

Her full lips flattened as she hummed. "'Know' is a strong word. They tend to keep to themselves."

"Do you have any idea where I could find them?" Arlon asked.

"They go into town a lot," she said as her eyes traced him. Like she was picking out every flaw on him. It made him itch. "But the weather's nice. They might be out in the transmutation yard."

"Thank you," he said and quickly tried to make his exit.

"Maybe after you find them, you could come find me, too. My name's Magda."

Arlon whirled, and for once, it was his turn to stare. So many of his interactions with people outside of Vian's pack had ended in an argument, a fight, or worse, but Magda looked at him with a very different sort of heat in her amber eyes.

She must have read his stunned silence as an invitation, because she stepped towards him. Her hips swayed as she approached, and under his shock, a part of him recognized just how beautiful she was. Her skin was like polished walnut, and though she was barely half his height, she carried herself like the tallest person in the room. Her hands lifted to trail down his chest, toying with the collar of his shirt. When she looked up at him, she held her lower lip coyly between her pearly teeth.

"I've been curious to see how the Wolf makes magic."

His embarrassment flashed to shame before landing on a resigned sort of anger. He suddenly understood what lay behind the stares, and he didn't like it. To any one of these nobles or highborns, he was an idea, and a titillating one at that. A dangerous sort of conquest. A villain for their fantasies.

He grabbed Magda's wrists, pulling her hands away from him before he lifted them over her head. Her eyes went wide, her smile turning hungry as he stepped her back. She let out a quiet gasp as her back hit the stone wall, her hands clenching to fists in his grip as he pinned them over her head.

"You don't know what you're asking," Arlon growled, but if he thought intimidation would make her back down, he was mistaken. It only seemed to stoke the fire of her fantasy.

"I think I do," Magda said, breathless with excitement.

He sneered down at her before he roughly released her wrists. "No, you don't," he said shortly. He turned to find the quickest route to the transmutation yard before he said or did something he regretted. He could almost feel Magda's baffled gaze following him and was grateful when he descended the stairs out of her sight.

The whole interaction made his skin itch, a sour feeling settling in his stomach. It left him in a poor mood he couldn't seem to shake, but at least Magda's tip paid off. As he stepped through the archway to the transmutation courtyard, he finally caught sight of the wizards he was looking for.

Among the well-bred nobility of the Crux, they seemed... familiar in a way that Arlon wasn't expecting.

Garrett sat in the grass, skin as gray as a storm cloud, his face made of hard angles that were not quite human. An orc, or at least part one like Arlon's pack-mate Pashka had been. He was a tough-looking man, his nose ridged like it had been broken more than once, but his slate-gray eyes looked fondly down at the woman whose head rested in his lap. Small tusks jutted up from behind his smiling bottom lip.

Where he seemed made of rock and earth, Bridgette

seemed to be made of starlight. She was beautiful, skin as pale and smooth as marble with hair like spun silver. She toyed with the end of Garrett's long braid as she said something that Arlon couldn't hear. It made Garrett laugh, a deep, resonant sound that only dissipated when he leaned down to kiss the woman reclining against him.

It felt like a private moment. Something between lovers. Something not meant for him. The sour feeling that Magda had left him with solidified to stone. Arlon left before either of them even noticed him.

Yet days passed without so much of a glimpse of them, and Arlon began to feel like he'd lost his chance. They didn't take meals in the mess hall, didn't seem to use the baths at normal times. Arlon didn't like lingering in the common areas, but Fawn had refused to even tell him which tower their rooms were in, so he didn't have another choice.

Grudgingly, Arlon grabbed his loaned copy of *Fundamentals of Magic* and used it as an excuse to sit in the shade of the transmutation yard. It felt like loitering. It *was* loitering, and he had to remind himself that he was *allowed* to be here, dammit.

The Wolves hadn't been welcomed anywhere. Trying to insert yourself into places you didn't belong earned you contempt or worse. Arlon found a compromise and made himself as unobtrusive as possible, choosing a spot on the grass against the far wall.

A week later, his patience finally paid off. Well, kind of. Instead of meeting the two wizards as they entered the transmutation yard, Garrett and Bridgette had beat him there.

"Thumb on the *outside* of your fist," the man's deep voice rumbled. "Fingers tight. Yup, there you go. Now, throw it like you mean it."

Bridgette scrunched her face up as she let her fist fly. It slapped against the man's big palm, but the strength behind her attack carried the rest of her forward. It put her off balance, and she yelped as Garrett caught her around the waist to pull her flush against him.

"Love your enthusiasm," Garrett chuckled. "But throw your *fist*, not your shoulder. Remember to keep those feet wide and drop your center down."

"Poor instruction," she laughed, face flushed before she caught sight of Arlon. She cleared her throat as she straightened her skirts out, though she couldn't quite wipe the smile from her face. "Sorry. You can use the yard if you want. We're not doing anything important."

"No, it's alright," Arlon said. He felt so awkward that it was nearly painful, but he forced the polite question out anyway. "Are you two sparring?"

The gray-skinned man gave a sly grin. "That's a strong word for it."

"Ass!" the woman said through a laugh as she shoved him away. "You're the one who insisted on this little lesson." She brushed a strand of silver-white hair behind her ear as she turned to grin at Arlon. "I'm Bridgette." She jerked a thumb at her companion. "This is my husband, Garrett."

"Arlon," he said as he studied her face. She was even more beautiful up close, but something about her tugged at a memory. Yet it wasn't until Bridgette's blue eyes sharpened to a glare that he realized *where* he had seen her before.

"I know you," she said, voice hardening.

The realization dropped like a stone. It felt like a lifetime ago that Vian and his Wolves had paid their last visit to Frostcliff. The brothel had been warm and welcoming, but like so many of the brothels in the mountains, it had an air of desperation about it. One that had made Arlon take very little interest in the offerings.

But Vian had.

He'd gone upstairs with a beautiful, silver-haired woman and returned with a bloodied knife.

That same woman glared at him now. She crossed her arms over her chest and took a step away from Arlon. "You're the Wolf."

The title felt like a stain that he couldn't get rid of, yet unlike the interest he'd garnered from Magda, the immediate hatred was familiar. It was the rejection he'd been bracing for the past two months, and hearing it so plainly in Bridgette's voice made it easy to return to old habits.

He bared his teeth in a grin. "What of it? Afraid you'll get eaten?"

He sounded like Vian. The man had always been a braggart, and even now, Arlon remembered every word of what he'd boasted as they fled the busy brothel that night.

Drew three lines down her thigh with my knife, and she never even screamed. Tough little whore.

The idea of taking one of Vian's Wolves to bed may have been an exciting idea to these highborns, but the reality of all the terror and grief his former boss had wrought in the mountains lived on in Bridgette's eyes.

Garrett crossed his arms over his chest, moving to stand between the two of them. "How'd a Wolf get an invitation to the Crux?"

It was as if the past year with Fawn had never happened. Every lesson she'd imparted on him, every method she'd given to regulate his own temper, vanished. Arlon's hackles were already raised, and the only thing he could think to do was escalate. Hit back harder and faster. "Funny, I wondered the same thing about a mutt."

Garrett didn't seem phased by the insult. As if he'd heard it before. He probably had. His storm-gray eyes sized Arlon up before a smirk crossed his face.

"Your pack ever teach you to spar?" Garrett asked, his tone south of friendly. "Or did you just ambush?"

Arlon's grin felt closer to a snarl. "You want to find out?"

Garrett motioned him forward with two fingers. "Didn't get to at Monika's. Would have really liked to."

"Garrett," Bridgette said in warning.

As they locked eyes, an entire silent conversation seemed to take place. Bridgette raised an eyebrow, and a smirk tugged at her lips before she turned those piercing eyes expectantly onto Arlon.

Garrett flashed a toothy grin as he stepped forward to square off, and Arlon realized that for the first time in his life, he was about to fight someone his own godsdamned size.

Smaller opponents, no problem. Usually. Arlon had learned the hard way that size only mattered to a point with someone who knew how to fight. And just looking at him, Garrett undoubtedly *knew how to fight.* He was only a hair shorter than Arlon, but he made up for it in muscle, his Crux-supplied shirt stretched across a broad chest and bulging forearms.

Recognition hit him like a club. Garrett had been at the brothel that night, too. As *security.*

Garrett smirked before delivering a shove that forced Arlon back a step. "C'mon, let's see what you got, Arlon."

Some quiet part of him knew what a bad idea this was. Vian never *taught* anyone to fight. You learned on the job. If you didn't, you ended up dead on the side of the road, just like his pack-mate Pashka had.

A thought that sounded very much like Fawn reminded him he was supposed to be making *friends,* dammit, but the Wolf had been summoned, and when it lunged, Arlon's feet were the ones to move. A growl rumbled from his throat as he brought his fist around, aiming for Garrett's braided head.

And missed. Badly.

Garrett stepped out of the way. One easy adjustment, like Arlon's attack had come in slow motion.

Arlon lunged again and again, and as the man effortlessly sidestepped a third time, the Wolf suddenly cowered as Arlon's own common fucking sense snapped back into place.

Get humbled, idiot. Hope he doesn't kill you.

Pain flared from his ribs as Garrett's fist connected like a boulder, knocking the wind clean out of him. He barely had time to cough before he was on the ground, face pressed into the damp grass. A weight descended on him, hot and oppressive. His right arm was yanked behind him, and his shoulder screamed as the joint locked.

Panic flared hot, bile rising in the back of Arlon's throat. His feet scrambled across the grass, searching for purchase and finding none. Memories stirred from a dark, recessed part of his mind, and for one horrifying moment, it felt like Vian was still alive.

Arlon's voice emerged choked and afraid. "Stop. Stop! STOP!"

Garrett's weight lifted off him in a heartbeat, and as that simple demand was met, Arlon snapped back to himself, already halfway to his feet. He staggered, wiping grass from his cheek. Something like concern crossed Garrett's face, but Arlon barely saw it through his own shame and mortification.

"Are you al—"

Without a word, Arlon fled for the atrium. A Wolf with his tail tucked.

4

"What happened?"

Arlon stared up at the ceiling, unblinking. The magiline that made up the walls of Fawn's quarters was illuminated by candlelight, the curtains of her bed waving gently in the cool spring air.

It was oppressive as the silence descended. That godsdamned silence that seemed to pull words out of him like a fish on a hook. Anger sparked when she didn't back down, but instead of bottling it in, letting it infuse into one indiscernible mess of an emotion, Arlon picked out what was behind it.

"I fucked up."

Fawn hummed as she trailed a finger down his collar to find the v of his shirt. "How?"

Arlon lifted his hands, pressing his palms against his eyes until he saw blots of color. He couldn't stand to look at her, see her disappointment. "Talked to Garrett and Bridgette."

Something teasing slipped into Fawn's tone as she said, "That, in and of itself, does not seem like a fuck up."

"They knew who I was," Arlon said.

"No, they didn't." Her fingers traced the edge of the crescent-shaped scar that crossed his chest. It was all that remained of the wound she'd given him when she arrested him, but the gentleness of her touch made him shiver. "They knew your reputation."

"Intimately." Fawn must have sensed something in his voice because the silence descended again until Arlon found the words to break it. "Bridgette and Garrett crossed paths with the Wolves in Frostcliff. About a year and a half ago, Vian brought some of us to the brothel Bridgette used to work at. She took Vian upstairs, and he hurt her. Badly."

He could feel Fawn's surprise as she tensed against him. "What happened today?"

He felt unworthy of that endless patience. It was never *"What did you do?"* Never accusatory.

"When Bridgette realized who I was, I... got on my guard."

Fawn seemed to sense all he wasn't saying. "And then?"

Arlon shrugged, but Fawn cupped his face, gently urging until he turned his head to look at her. Concern pinched her eyebrows. "Tell me."

"Garrett challenged me to a spar. I accepted. And he beat me. Handily, even."

Fawn winced as her thumb stroked his cheek. "Ah. He told me that he's... capable in a fight."

"Can confirm that," Arlon said through a sigh. "So, I'm sorry, but I think your wizards hate me."

Fawn tsked. "They don't *know* you."

"Well, I showed my whole ass to them over a dirty look," Arlon muttered. "That's telling enough."

Fawn fell quiet as she looked at him, her blue eyes shining like a cat's in the dim light of her quarters. For once, she was the one who broke the silence. "Did something else happen?"

Arlon swallowed the knot that had suddenly formed in his throat. Fawn waited, her fingers stroking through his hair until he said, "When Garrett got me pinned, it felt like I was back in Vian's pack. Like I'd never left. Couldn't leave."

Fawn was quiet as she shifted to straddle his waist. Her comforting warmth settled onto him, her bare thighs hugging his waist as her hands rested against his chest. "Memories like yours are hard to forget. You shouldn't punish yourself for getting lost in them."

His hands found the curve of her waist, her naked skin glowing in the dim flicker of candlelight. After how he'd acted with Bridgette and Garrett, he suddenly felt unworthy to be in her presence. Everything he'd said and done felt like spitting in the face of Fawn's seemingly endless patience with him.

Little over a year ago, he would have never looked back at the interaction in the transmutation yard, but Fawn had changed the color of his world, and he didn't like the darkness he saw in himself.

"Would you punish me, then?"

Fawn's shining gaze sharpened as she looked down at him, considering. "I won't punish you for your past, Arlon. You can't change what you've been through. So, what exactly do you feel you need to be punished for?"

Her voice had hardened, taking on that tone that made him tremble. Under her gaze, he felt stripped bare. "I got defensive when I shouldn't have. I let my ego get the best of me. I-I had an opportunity to make friends, and I squandered it because I let a simple comment turn me into the person I'm *trying* not to be anymore."

Frustration made his voice shake, but Fawn brought him back as she cupped his cheek. "Then on your knees, *a'marra*. I'll remind you who you are."

Her weight lifted, and Arlon obeyed as he slid off the bed.

He sank to his knees on the stone floor, soaking in the safety of her presence as he lowered his head, hands clenched on the tops of his thighs. Fawn shifted until her legs hung off the side of the bed. She sat right in front of him, close enough that he could lean forward and kiss her knee.

One delicate foot came up to rest against his shoulder as she spread her legs. Her fingers wove through his hair before gripping tight. It was rough enough to make a few strands part with his scalp as she pulled him forward, trapping him firmly in the crux of her smooth thighs.

"You are brash, impatient," she said as his mouth found her entrance without thought, tongue darting out to taste her. "Willful and stubborn as an ox."

He clenched his eyes shut as he pressed his tongue into her, tasting, seeking, as if she was capable of giving him the answers about his own nature that he couldn't find himself. Her next words emerged on something like a moan. "You hide under an exterior of rock. One would think you don't *have* emotions with how little you show them."

As close as she held him, Arlon couldn't block out the words. Each one felt like a kick in the stomach, and he started to feel lightheaded from the truths she shot at him, the slow suffocation of her legs. He redoubled his efforts like a plea for mercy, his teeth gently grazing the folds of her cunt. Her hips jumped before he slid his tongue deep again, lips sucking gently.

"You let your ego speak when your rational mind should," Fawn said, her voice hitching as she ground down against his mouth. "You've been called a beast because of your past, and you proved them right."

He raised his hands, searching for her, but she slapped them away. "Hands behind your back. You can't hide here."

Arlon let out a quiet sound of anguish as he obeyed. He

clasped his arms behind him, holding onto his forearms to keep them folded. When she lifted his head, he gasped for breath, his cock aching as he looked up at her through tear-blurred eyes.

"Vicious. Violent. You hit first to avoid giving others the opportunity."

Arlon quaked, feeling stripped bare by every word. Because the fact was, they were all true. Every. Single. One.

Fawn's hands cupped his face, and Arlon flinched like he had been torn open. Her level blue eyes met his, her thumbs gentle as she stroked his cheek. She waited until his heaving breaths settled to a stutter before she continued.

"And everything you did..." Her tone had softened, but Arlon braced, holding himself like he expected to be hit. "Everything you did was to *protect* yourself, Arlon. Someone who has been struck again and again eventually learns to defend themselves."

His eyes spilled over, but Fawn didn't let him pull away. Her lips lifted into a gentle smile, and something in Arlon's chest unlocked as the torrent of guilt broke free, a rock face giving way to an avalanche.

"You are not a villain," she said. "You were forced to become one. Hurting is not in your nature. *Viciousness* is not in your nature. You are far too good and far too kind for the road you were made to walk down."

That part of him that sounded like Vian hissed that she was lying. That no whispered assurances could erase the stain left on his soul. The darkness tried to wrap its tendrils around his heart, harden him against the things she said, but it was like Fawn could feel it.

"You are no Wolf." He didn't know when he'd torn out of her grip to bury his face against her thigh until she cupped his chin, guiding him up so she could press a kiss against his forehead. "Do you believe me when I say that?"

Arlon grimaced as he met her shining eyes. He had been lied to so many times. Had been conditioned to second-guess every motive, every kindness.

But Fawn was the exception. Her black hair cascaded over her shoulders as she smiled down at him. She had never lied to him. Not even when he hadn't deserved the truth.

"I believe you."

Her arms circled him, pulling his head to rest against her as she kissed his hair. "And when I say you are worthy of love, worthy of friendship, do you still believe me?"

Fawn could read him like no one else could. Had seen him at his worst and had brought out his best. If she could see who he was through the stain of his past, then maybe others could, too.

"I believe you."

5

The next day, Arlon started his search for Garrett and Bridgette all over again. Yet this search ended much quicker when he bumped into the former while turning the corner to the main atrium. Arlon bounced off of his broad chest, but Garrett didn't so much as budge.

The other man grabbed his arm to steady him, but he let go just as quickly. As if Arlon was a hot pan he was eager to drop. "Shit, sorry."

"No, my fault," Arlon said. He tried to grin, but it felt forced. Felt like he didn't know how to do it right. He gave it up, falling into his usual, comfortable scowl.

"Actually, I'm glad I ran into you," Garrett said. "I... wanted to be sure you were alright. I was afraid I'd hurt you."

Arlon's shoulders relaxed a little. If he cared enough to be concerned, then maybe Garrett didn't *fully* hate him.

"No—no, I'm fine," Arlon assured him. He forced the next words out on a breath. "I wanted to apologize. I was an ass to you yesterday. To Bridgette, too. I'm sorry."

Garrett looked him over before he said, "Yeah, well. You

were the last person we expected to find in the Crux, but there must be a reason Fawn let you in."

"Yeah, well."

An awkward silence stretched between them before Garrett broke it. "How'd it happen?"

There was no use in trying to hide it. They already knew who he had been. He had to do as Fawn suggested and tell them who he was now.

"I was press-ganged into Vian's pack at sixteen. Stayed with him for a decade until Fawn arrested me. Served my sentence to the Crown, helped *kill* the evil fucker, and now I'm a wizard of the Crux, same as you."

Garrett's eyebrows shot up. "Woah, wait. Vian Wolf is *dead?*"

"For a little over two months, now," Arlon said, and his grin came a little easier this time. It was a nice reminder to have.

"Well fuck me," Garrett chuckled. "Shame I never got a shot at him, but I can't be mad he's gone."

"You could've taken him," Arlon huffed around a laugh. The tension in his shoulders eased some more. "How'd you learn to fight like that?"

Garrett shrugged as something unreadable crossed his face. "I've just had a lot of practice."

The words were out before Arlon could stop himself. "Would you teach me?"

Garrett blinked in surprise. "Seriously? Why?"

Arlon crossed his arms over his chest, averting his gaze. "I don't want to lose a fight like that again. Ever."

Garrett looked him over, slate-gray eyes searching. It was like they could see right through Arlon's mask to the fear underneath.

But Garrett must have understood something of fear

himself, because he said, "Alright, Arlon. I can give you some tips."

The next morning, Arlon headed down to meet Garrett in the evocation yard. Unlike the rest of the courtyards that were designed with comfort in mind, the evocation yard saw far rougher use. It contained nothing but a couple of wooden benches scattered around a patch of dirt. Dirt that Garrett was raking as Arlon stepped into the yard.

"Don't think you're going to save that grass," Arlon said, eying the sparse spring green trying to break through the hard-packed earth.

Garrett turned to face him with a grin. "No, but you'll be thankful I've broken the ground up a bit."

Arlon crossed his arms over his chest with a frown. "Why's that?"

"Because I'm going to teach you how to fall."

Arlon raised an eyebrow. "Thought you were going to teach me to fight."

"You're asking to get hurt if you pick a fight without knowing how to go down first."

It wasn't the lesson he'd expected, but Arlon could see the wisdom in it. Garrett demonstrated first, doing a back fall and side fall that he made look easy before he instructed Arlon to try. The first back fall he attempted knocked the wind out of him. The second was little better, but Garrett was patient and helpful, giving him tips like "tuck your chin" and "slap the ground *as* you connect, not after."

As the morning passed, Arlon was very, very grateful that

Garrett had softened the ground up a bit. When they finally called it quits at the lunch bell, he was sporting new bruises on his hips, but not nearly as many as he would have without Garrett's forethought.

"Same time tomorrow?" Garrett asked with a bright grin.

Arlon tried not to let his annoyance show. "You going to actually teach me how to fight?"

Garrett chuckled as he looked him over. "We'll see."

The next morning, Arlon woke with regrets. He was as sore as the day after he'd been initiated into the Wolves. For a moment, he debated skipping out on Garrett's lesson, but something stopped him. Maybe it was his competitive streak, some ingrained stubbornness, or maybe... a part of him had enjoyed the other man's company yesterday.

No matter what it was, he hauled his sore body out of bed and went down to meet Garrett in the evocation yard once more.

"How you feeling?" Garrett asked.

"Last time I hurt this much, I at least had the excuse of having the shit kicked out of me," Arlon admitted.

Garrett barked a laugh, and the sound tugged at the corner of Arlon's lips.

"I'll take pity on you today," Garrett said. "Let's see your fighting stance."

Arlon showed him, spreading his legs a shoulder's length apart and dropping his weight down. Garrett circled around him before he tapped his left thigh until Arlon moved it back and out. It put the majority of his weight on his front leg, and Garrett used one of his own to correct the position of Arlon's back foot.

"That's a front stance," Garrett said before he tapped Arlon's legs again until he moved them into more of an L shape. It felt awkward before Garrett tapped the back of his knee until he bent it. "That's a back stance. Now spread your legs a little wider than your shoulders. Good, now drop your butt down. That's a horse stance."

Garrett showed him how to step while keeping his stance, and together, they moved back and forth across the yard in steady, measured steps. Every time Arlon slipped out of his stance, Garrett would correct him with a gentle tap to the offending spot. They continued until his thighs burned, and it was only Arlon's competitiveness that kept him moving right alongside Garrett until the lunch bell rang.

"This is... not what I expected... when you said you'd... give me fighting tips," Arlon panted as he sprawled in the shade of the wall to give his aching legs a rest. It wasn't terribly hot out, but his shirt was soaked all the same. Garrett sat on the ground beside him, and seeing how he'd barely broken a sweat, it was hard to believe they'd both spent the morning doing the same damn thing.

"You've been relying on raw strength, and it shows," Garrett said. "You've got some bad habits to unlearn."

"Is that why I'm so sore? You have to beat the bad habits out of me?"

Garrett barked a laugh. "I haven't beat anything out of you yet. We'll start that tomorrow."

And they sure did. The next morning, Garrett showed him a range of arm and leg blocks that he drilled into him until Arlon had bruises coating his forearms and shins. But each bruise was a lesson learned, and being able to stop an attack made him feel like maybe he was actually starting to learn something.

It wasn't until a couple days later, nearly a full week into the start of their new training regimen, that Garrett finally taught him some strikes. Nothing fancy, simple punches and kicks, but Garrett's focus on good technique and form was a marked difference from the "instruction" he'd gotten from Vian and the other Wolves.

Garrett taught him how to keep a tight fist, what part of his hand and foot to strike with so he didn't hurt himself. Garrett had him combine the simple strikes in conjunction with the movements he'd taught him earlier in the week. Moving with the right stance helped give power to the strikes, and all the time they'd spent ingraining the motions into Arlon's muscles paid off.

With a solid foundation starting to form, Garrett slowly built him up as days turned to weeks. Trips, hip throws, shoulder throws, takedowns. Each new technique Arlon learned stacked on top of something that Garrett had already taught him. Then, one morning, after they finished their warmups, Garrett stood opposite of Arlon and motioned him forward with two fingers.

"Spar with me."

Arlon stared at the bare-chested man in surprise. Even though this was the whole reason he had asked Garrett to teach him in the first place, he hesitated now.

"You sure?" Arlon asked.

Garrett smirked. "Afraid you'll win? Don't be."

"Ass," Arlon chuckled. "More afraid of you pounding me into the dirt again."

"Valid fear," Garrett said. "But we both know I don't have anything to prove. I just want to see what you've picked up. Pull your strikes and kicks, and don't aim for the crotch or head. This is a friendly spar."

Arlon squared off with the man as he brought his fists up. "You saying we're friends now?"

"Aren't we?" Garrett asked before he lashed out with a side kick.

The question threw him, but Arlon's hard-earned muscle

memory kicked in automatically. He blocked with a forearm before he sidestepped in to try and bring a knee to Garrett's middle.

The man hooked one arm under Arlon's raised leg before he tripped his other one out from under him. Arlon went down with a grunt and understood immediately why Garrett had spent days drilling falls into him. The impact rattled his bones, but it was Garrett's weight on top of him that made old fears jolt to life.

Before that panic could even set in, Garrett was off of him, offering him a hand up. "That was a good block." Arlon took his hand, a little stunned as the man pulled him to his feet, clapping him on the shoulder. "Want to try it again?"

"I—yeah. Sure."

Garrett hadn't been idly boasting. Arlon lost many, *many* more times. No matter how strong of a stance Arlon adopted, how well he distributed his weight, within a few strikes, Garrett found an opening and got him on the ground with ease.

The fear of being overpowered dwindled the more it happened. By the time they stopped at the lunch bell, they were both a little more scuffed and bruised, and Arlon was too tired to be afraid. After the last takedown, Arlon stayed on the ground even after Garrett got up.

"You're definitely picking things up," Garrett said, and Arlon was satisfied that the man at least sounded a little winded.

"Where the hell did you learn how to fight?" Arlon asked as he tried to rub away the dirt that stuck to his sweaty arms. It was a losing task.

Garrett grabbed the waterskin and took a long sip before he said, "My mother taught me. She's the best warrior my clan has ever seen. Passed those lessons onto me whether I wanted them or not."

"I'm seeing the family resemblance."

Garrett chuckled and said, "You can walk any time you want. Or did you forget that you asked for this?"

"Guess I did," Arlon said with a grin. "Was expecting some tips, not an entire godsdamned retraining."

"Gotta actually *have* some training before you can be retrained," Garrett teased, and Arlon reached out with one leg to deliver a half-hearted kick. "You want to hit the baths? I feel like I'm making mud sitting here."

The question made Arlon pause. Being fully naked made him uneasy for a lot of reasons. Even while fucking or casting with Fawn, he liked having that small bit of armor, but to go to the baths, shedding his clothes was a necessity.

But after today, his hesitation felt silly. Garrett had overpowered him countless times without hurting him. Every time Arlon tapped, Garrett respected it, and that alone made the other man feel... safe.

Besides all that, Garrett had called them friends, and the word had settled like a ball of warmth in his chest.

"Yeah, let's go."

Garrett offered him a hand up, and Arlon took it. They walked in a comfortable silence through the atrium, but as they reached the hallway through the main tower, Fawn emerged from her office. She was likely on her way to lunch, but she looked them over as she approached, taking in the significant amount of dirt that clung to them.

"Is your fighting club drawing blood now?" she asked, looking pointedly at Arlon's knees that were caked with a bit of dried blood and dirt. She'd seen plenty of bruises on him since Garrett started training him, but this was the first time he'd earned anything more. It felt like a strange point of pride.

"We were just going to wash off," Arlon said.

"That was my fault," Garrett said quickly. "Keep forgetting we're sparring on dirt instead of a mat."

Fawn hummed as she looked between the two of them. "What kind of mat?"

Garrett rubbed the back of his neck. He seemed a little flustered, and Arlon wondered how much experience he had with the Grandmaster. Going off the wide-eyed look he gave her, it wasn't much.

"Um, we used to weave them out of yak fur in my clan," Garrett said. "But dirt's not so bad. At least the evocation yard isn't gravel."

"Gods, that makes me hurt just thinking about it," Arlon muttered.

Fawn hummed again, amusement dancing in her eyes. "Let me see if I can't find you something softer than dirt to land on."

"Oh," Garrett said in surprise. "Thank you, Grandmaster."

Fawn leaned up to kiss Arlon's cheek. "Enjoy your bath."

The pride in her smile warmed him, and as he and Garrett continued down the hall, Arlon couldn't shed the grin that tugged at his lips.

Garrett waited until they were surrounded by the steam of the baths before he broke the silence. "I heard the rumor that you were... close with the Grandmaster."

Arlon turned away from him and checked to be sure the baths were empty before he lifted his shirt off. He'd always been self-conscious about his size, but being side by side with Garrett, when the man was just as big and scarred as he was, made him feel a little silly.

"I am."

He shed his shoes and pants just as quickly before he slipped into the relative cover of the water. It stung every scrape on him, but he let out a sigh of relief at the heat.

Garrett joined him a moment later, and as the other man sank to sit on the bench across from him, Arlon couldn't help but appreciate the way his muscles moved.

"Sorry if that was a weird question," Garrett said. "I get that it's how magic is made, but I'm still getting used to the thought that everyone I talk to is fucking in some way or another."

Arlon let out a huff of a laugh. "Don't have to worry about that with me. I've only ever made magic with Fawn."

"Same with me and Bridgette," Garrett said. "She's starting to branch out a bit, but... I don't know."

"Haven't found anyone you want to fuck around with?" Arlon teased.

Garrett's eyes darted to Arlon before darting away just as quickly. "I wouldn't say that." He gave a wry grin as he crossed his arms over his chest. "Gods know the Crux has no lack of attractive people."

Arlon looked at the other man curiously. "You and Bridgette are married, right?"

"Yup."

"Does it bother you that she's casting with others?" Arlon asked.

"No," Garrett chuckled. "You know where she worked before here. Now, instead of just imagining what she did with her clients upstairs, I get to watch."

Arlon swallowed, his mouth suddenly dry. Something about that idea embedded in his head—both of them. He was grateful the water hid how his cock twitched.

Garrett didn't seem to notice as he leaned back before scooping water up to wash the dirt from his chest. "You don't have to answer this, but why haven't you cast with anyone else?"

Arlon sank a little further into the water and crossed his

arms over his chest, remembering the awkward moment he'd had with Magda a few weeks ago. "They look at me and see a Wolf. I'm not interested in being that for anyone, even as a fantasy."

Garrett tsked in sympathy. "No, I get it. A couple months after Bri and I got here, this pretty little noble—I think her name was Sabine? She asked if I wanted to take her as my *war bride* for the night."

"Fuck. That's a hell of a way to say hello."

"That's what I thought," Garrett chuckled as he started to unwind his long braid. "Needless to say, Sabine went to bed unconquered that night." He finished freeing his hair before he sank further into the water, wetting the strands until they hung straight down his back. His tone sobered a little as he said, "It kinda... I don't know. Messed with my head a bit. I *like* the idea of making magic with others, but..."

Arlon grabbed a washcloth to help scrub the dirt and blood from the scrapes on his knees. "I get it. Magda said she wanted to see how the Wolf made magic and I just..." He sighed. "If I'm going to fuck around, it's going to be with people who see me as a person, not just some fantasy."

Garrett let out a long breath as he sank down, letting his head rest against the lip of the pool. "Here, here."

He seemed completely at ease in Arlon's company, and it was a nice surprise to realize that Arlon felt the same way. It didn't feel weighted or awkward being naked around the other man, and he sank a little more comfortably into the water to just enjoy it. They soaked in a companionable silence until chatter sounded at the top of the stairs. With a shared look, they came to an unspoken agreement before they got out and got dressed.

"See you tomorrow morning?" Garrett asked as he re-braided his wet hair.

It was an easy answer. "Yeah, see you then."

6

The familiar nightmare always started with the smell of damp earth. It filled his nose, cutting through the fog of liquor that had clouded his head that night. As it always did, the hauntingly familiar weight settled on top of him. He fought it on instinct, but the weight only seemed to grow, bearing down on him, as inescapable and inevitable as nightfall. Hot breath tickled his ear as he was overpowered, before a hand clamped over the back of his neck.

Quiet, boy. Don't want to wake the camp, do you?

Arlon jolted awake, the echo of Vian's voice still in his ear. For a moment, he just stared at the moonlight streaming in through his window as he tried to wrestle his racing heart back under control. His modest room felt oppressive in the wake of the dream. Too dark, too quiet.

It was too late for regrets, but a part of him wished he could go back to earlier in the evening and ask Fawn if he could sleep in her quarters with her. Maybe if he had, the old nightmare would have stayed away. Ever since Vian's death, he had thought he had finally escaped this particular dream, and it rattled him to be proved so wrong.

He tossed his blankets off and got up, pulling a shirt on over his sleeping shorts. Fawn had assured him that there was no place in the Crux he wasn't welcome, and he hoped that remained true when he knocked on her door at whatever godsforsaken hour it was. Trying to return to sleep in his own bed felt like tempting Vian's ghost to visit again.

Instead, he went to his door and threw it open, only to earn a startled gasp from someone just outside.

It was Bridgette, a light globe clasped in her hand. She was backed against the far wall, one hand on her chest, her blue eyes wide with alarm.

"Gods, you scared the shit out of me," she hissed, keeping her voice to a whisper.

"Sorry," Arlon said, equally surprised to see someone else up this late. Yet some small part of him found it funny that he'd spent so many days searching for Garrett and Bridgette when at least Bridgette shared a floor with him.

The woman looked him over before she asked, "You alright? You look about how I felt when I thought you were a fucking ghost."

Arlon swore and rubbed his tired eyes. "I—no, I'm fine. Couldn't sleep."

Bridgette frowned as some silent battle played out behind her eyes. Finally, she sighed and said, "I couldn't sleep, either. I was going to go for a walk if you want to come?"

Frankly, Arlon was shocked she wanted anything to do with him. Especially something that involved being alone with him in the middle of the night.

It was like she could read his thoughts. She pulled a strand of spells out from under her nightgown. "I'm not stupid enough to go walking around in the dark without a little assurance."

Something about her tone wrung a quiet huff from him. The woman was an uncomfortable reminder of who he used to be, but that wasn't *her* fault. No doubt he was a reminder of something she'd rather forget, too, so the fact that she had even asked him to join felt significant. A tenuous sort of peace offering.

"You sure you want company?"

"Look, my husband likes you. I should give you the benefit of the doubt and at least *try*," she said matter-of-factly. Her eyes scanned over him again, appraising. "Besides, you're the one who looks like you could use some company."

He really, really did. Even now, his heart raced, still trying to escape the long-dead threat of Vian Wolf.

Bridgette hummed, reading his silence, before she jerked her head towards the stairs. "C'mon then."

Arlon obeyed the command and fell into step beside her. She led them down the stairs of the abjuration tower and through the main atrium before cutting towards the transmutation yard. It seemed to be a familiar route for her, and Arlon was glad to only have to think about putting one foot in front of the other.

"I've been meaning to thank you," Bridgette said as they emerged into the yard, finally breaking the silence that hung between them.

"For what?" Arlon asked, not quite able to hide his surprise.

Bridgette shrugged as she reached into her pocket and pulled out a small clay pipe. "Garrett has had a harder time settling in here than I have. Your sparring sessions have helped."

She walked over to the pagoda of woven trees before she

took a seat on the bench underneath them. A match sparked against the side of the clay pipe before Bridgette lit its contents. She drew out a few puffs, and Arlon caught the familiar scent of tobacco and skunkweed.

"You want any? It helps me sleep when I'm having a rough night," she said as she held the pipe out to him, smoke pouring from her lips.

Arlon eyed the offering before he took it. The clay pipe was comically small in his hand, but he filled his lungs with smoke before letting it out on a sigh.

"Fuck," he murmured, the familiar taste plucking at a few good memories from his time with the Wolves. How many late nights had he spent smoking around a campfire, bullshitting about everything and nothing?

"Good, right?" Bridgette said, grinning as she took the pipe back. "Came from this apothecary in town. Far nicer than anything I ever found in Frostcliff."

Arlon handed the pipe back to her before he took a seat on the bench next to her. "Do you ever miss Frostcliff?"

To his surprise, Bridgette laughed. "*Gods* no. Not even a little bit. Frostcliff is a shithole compared to Straetham."

Arlon chuckled as she took another puff out of the pipe. "Frostcliff wasn't so bad."

Bridgette released a plume of smoke into the air before handing the pipe back to him. "Spoken like someone who could come and go as he pleased."

Arlon scoffed before he drew in a deep breath, the smoke dancing over his tongue. It felt strange to smoke without a drink in hand, but the nightmare was a good reminder of why he'd never touch a drop again. "We didn't come and go, we snuck in and fled once we overstayed our welcome. That's what happens when you're wanted in damn near every town in the Hobokins."

Bridgette hummed as she took the pipe back from him. "Garrett told me that you were with the Wolves for some time."

He should have assumed this was where the conversation was going. It seemed like there was no escaping the thought of Vian tonight. "Too long."

"How'd you fall in with them?"

Arlon sighed, and maybe it was the comfortable haze of the skunkweed that loosened his tongue enough to say, "It was the worst day of my life. You really want to hear about it?"

Another curl of smoke left Bridgette's mouth, and she folded one knee, laying it across the top of the bench so she could turn to face him. "I'll tell you mine if you tell me yours."

Arlon raised an eyebrow but took the offered pipe all the same. He drew in a fortifying lungful of smoke before he said, "That morning, I'd lit my mother's funeral pyre. That afternoon, I lost my home when my caravan kicked me out."

Bridgette was silent as he took another long drag on the pipe before saying, "That evening, Vian and his pack caught up to me on the road. Tried to rob me. I had a death wish and nothing to lose, so I fought back. Vian later told me that he liked my *tenacity*." He spit the word like venom. "Instead of leaving me for dead, they took me back to their camp."

"Gods, Arlon." Bridgette's voice was filled with equal parts horror and sympathy. "How old were you?"

Arlon handed the pipe back to her, not quite able to meet her eyes. "Sixteen."

Bridgette scoffed, cradling the pipe in her lap. "Sixteen's a cursed age."

"Why do you say that?"

"That's how old I was when my da sold me to that godsforsaken brothel to pay off his gambling debts," Bridgette murmured.

Arlon looked at the woman in surprise. Her head was lowered, her long silver hair cascading over her shoulders to obscure her face.

"You said you'd tell me yours," Arlon said after a moment. "Was that your worst day?"

"No." Bridgette lifted her eyes to meet his, and Arlon recognized something of the pain and anger that lingered in them. "That was the night I took your old boss upstairs."

Arlon's stomach plummeted. "I-I'm sorry." It felt inadequate. It *was* inadequate. There was nothing he could say or do that would heal the wounds Vian had left, but he still felt the need to try. "He was an evil fucker. He hurt a lot of people, and I'm sorry you were one of them."

Bridgette's eyes studied him, and it was like she could see all that he wasn't saying. "You were hurt by him, too."

He forced a smile, a weak, fragile thing. "A close second for worst day of my life."

Bridgette's wavering smile matched his. "Well, he's dead now, right?"

Arlon sighed, his shoulders relaxing a little. "He is."

"Well, then. Cheers to one less evil fucker in the world," Bridgette said before she held the pipe out to him.

His fingers brushed hers as he took it. "That story's a happier one, if you want to hear it."

Bridgette chuckled as she leaned back comfortably. "Go on, then. Tell me a happy tale."

Arlon took another draw from the pipe, grinning as he released the plume of smoke into the night sky. "After Fawn arrested me and a few of the others, I think Vian got desperate. He'd already proven himself a big enough problem to warrant the Crux's intervention, but after his Wolves got thinned, he started killing more readily, got more brutal with his extortions. But he was no less careful about covering his tracks.

For the entire year I was indentured here, Fawn was trying to track him down, without luck."

"So what made you decide to help?" Bridgette asked as she took the pipe back.

"Fawn promised me a clean slate and a new life as a wizard, to start."

"And?"

"And... after a year of helping me recognize all the ways Vian had fucked my life up, I *wanted* to help," he said.

Bridgette hummed as she tapped the ashes out of her pipe. "You're also in love with her." Arlon's stomach plummeted, but at his look, Bridgette scoffed. "I have eyes, you know."

Arlon cleared his throat, forcing that thought aside, though his racing heart took a moment longer to settle. "Anyway, I gave her the location of every hideout I knew of under the condition that I got to come with her to clear them. We caught up to Vian at the tail end of winter, and I don't think I need to tell you that a prick with a sword, even one as vicious as Vian Wolf, was no match for a fully armed wizard."

Bridgette leaned back with a smirk as she looked up at the sky. "Bet it was satisfying to watch him try."

"It was the only time I ever saw him afraid," Arlon said. "And knowing that he died feeling even a fraction of the fear he'd caused throughout his miserable life was good enough for me."

"A deserving end," Bridgette said before she spat on the ground next to her. "Hope Quietus sent him straight to hell where he belongs."

Arlon copied the sentiment, spitting onto the grass. "Without a doubt."

The silence that fell between them was a comfortable one. One that was only broken when Bridgette let out a wistful sigh as she got to her feet. "That *was* a happy story. I think I'll sleep better for having heard it."

Arlon would too, but he didn't admit it out loud. Instead, he said, "Thanks for... this."

Bridgette gave him an appraising look before she said, "Walk me back upstairs?"

Arlon got to his feet, and Bridgette slid her arm through his. The warmth of her touch was a surprise, but not an unwelcome one. They walked arm in arm all the way back to her room in the abjuration tower, which was, in fact, just a few doors down from his.

"Goodnight, Arlon," she whispered as she opened her door. "Sleep well."

"Yeah, you too."

7

"Are you alright, Arlon?"

"I'm alright, I'm alright."

Fawn cupped his chin, pulling his face up. A frown tugged at her lips. "You don't seem alright."

Arlon groaned and closed his eyes. That frown was hard to bear right now, because dammit, he was *trying*. In spite of the pillow, his knees ached where he knelt, but the ropes binding his thighs and shins didn't allow him to unfold. More ropes pulled his arms behind his back. They were no less constricting, chafing his wrists as he squirmed against them without thought.

"I asked for this," he said.

"And as with any other time you conduit, you're allowed to *stop*," she said.

Arlon vainly tried to sink into the embrace of the ropes rather than fight against them. "I need to learn how to conduit, right?"

"It *is* important that a caster knows what they're putting their conduits through," Fawn said. "But if you're not comfortable with conduiting, we can find other ways to teach you."

Arlon pulled his chin from her grip as he shook his head. Tapping out sounded tempting, but if he wanted to gain mastery in *any* school, he had to at least try.

"Stubborn," Fawn said, amusement coloring the word.

"Fawn, this is all I have."

His tone emerged sharper than intended, and Fawn didn't miss it. She knelt in front of him as she cupped his face. Her thumbs were gentle, stroking his cheeks in a comforting caress. "What do you mean, *a'marra*?"

Arlon swallowed, his frustration making his voice tremble as she forced him to meet her eyes. "I-I don't have anything outside of this place. Not anymore." He let out a long breath, trying to calm his racing thoughts enough to speak. "I want to be good at this. I *need* to be good at this."

Fawn was quiet as she considered him. "That's a lot of pressure to put on yourself."

"I-I know."

Fawn tilted her head curiously before an idea seemed to light in her eyes. "What do you find so enjoyable about casting?"

He thought on the question as he shifted in his ropes, trying to settle his knees more comfortably against the soft pillow underneath them. Finally, he said, "I like being in control."

Fawn hummed, her hands stroking down his neck, across his shoulders to the ropes that circled his forearms. "Then command me."

He blinked in surprise as gooseflesh shivered across his skin in the wake of her touch. "What?"

"Command me," Fawn said again as her hands stroked over his collarbone, just teasing at the v of his shirt. "Because let me be very clear about something, Arlon. Casters only have as much control as their conduits give them."

Arlon's mouth went dry as he studied her face. Her desire was written plainly across her features, but her touches remained innocent, waiting for his command.

"Stroke your hands under my shirt."

Fawn shifted closer to him, one of her knees brushing against his as she shared his pillow. Obligingly, she moved to the hem of his shirt. Her hands teased under the fabric, moving over his stomach to travel up through the hair on his chest as she thumbed over his nipples.

In spite of his unease, pleasure shivered through him. "Keep going. Use your mouth, too."

Fawn obeyed, her nails scratching gently down his chest as she leaned forward to kiss his exposed collar. Arlon groaned, bowing over her to bury his face against her neck, breathing in the lingering scent of juniper soap. Even while bound, her touch was a conditioned thing, and he relaxed by degrees as she nipped along his neck and chest.

"May I lift your shirt?" she asked.

"Yes," he breathed as he gently kissed her neck, just over her pulse.

Fawn shifted back, lifting his shirt up until it bunched under his bound arms. It exposed his chest, and she kissed the skin just over his heart before moving to tease one nipple with her tongue.

Arlon groaned as his trousers grew tight. He'd chosen to remain clothed for this conduiting lesson, but he was starting to have second thoughts about that particular demand.

"Touch my cock."

Fawn's fingers trailed down his stomach once more as her mouth moved to his other nipple. She cast her eyes up, giving him a mischievous look as she rubbed his cock through the fabric of his trousers. As firmly as she handled him, it wasn't enough to do anything more than tease him, and she seemed to know it.

"Fawn," he groaned, straining against his ropes as he tried to press into her hand.

"That was not a very specific demand," she teased before she toyed with the laces of his trousers. "Do you want me to loosen these?"

"Yes," he hissed, the ropes biting gently as he tried to roll his hips to meet her.

"As you command," Fawn said before she pulled his laces, plucking them loose until the bulge of his cock was contained by nothing but his underthings. Fawn cupped him again, and the touch was only slightly more satisfying as she traced the outline of his hardening cock.

A low growl emerged from his throat. "Such a tease. If I had my hands free—"

"But you don't," Fawn reminded him as she moved her hands to drape them over his shoulders. One of her knees slipped between his bound legs to rub his trapped cock. "So how would you like me to continue?"

Arlon groaned, and even as tightly as he was bound, he was able to grind against her knee. "I want to feel your hand around me. I want you to stroke me."

Fawn slipped a hand down between them, and Arlon groaned as she freed his length from his underthings. It only took her skin brushing his for him to harden fully. He pursed his lips to stop the sound of need that threatened to escape him as he vainly tried to thrust up to meet her. But her strokes remained slow and steady, spreading the precum that had started to bead on the tip of his cock.

"Faster," he ordered, and Fawn obeyed. As her hand sped up, Arlon buried his face against her neck, lips pressed against her skin to muffle his moan. He jerked and shuddered in her grip, sweat beading on his brow.

"You know control, *a'marra*," Fawn said, lips murmuring against his hair. "Would you like me to show you surrender?"

"Yes," he moaned, his end creeping ever near.

Fawn smiled against his hair, her hand expertly bringing him to the brink of pleasure.

And then she released him.

Arlon didn't recognize the ragged sound of disappointment that escaped his throat. He was ready to grab Fawn, pull her against him and not let her go. But he couldn't. The ropes held him helpless, and he had no choice but to sink into them, trembling.

"Fawn..."

Her chuckle sent shivers down his back. "Would you like me to keep going?"

"Yes," he panted, only to groan as Fawn wrapped her hand around his aching length again. This time, lube coated her hand, and he couldn't think of when she had grabbed it. He also couldn't bring himself to care, not with how good she felt as she tugged his length in firm strokes.

He tensed as she brought him to the edge again, only to pull her hand away once more.

"Fuck," he hissed as he sagged in the ropes, chest heaving. "Fawn, please."

"Please, what, *a'marra*?"

He bit back a groan as one finger circled the swollen head of his cock. "Make me cum."

Fawn hummed as her hand wrapped around his length again. He shuddered, eyes rolling closed as he strained to try and meet her. His thighs burned, his arms aching, but the ropes had become an afterthought. He kept his face against her neck, his breaths puffing against her skin as she toyed with him.

She played his body like an expert, hand speeding up and slowing down to keep him aching for release. He lost track of time, his attention focused on the feel of her hand, the gentle encouragements she murmured into his ear. It took him a second longer to realize that the quiet "please, please, please" was coming from his own lips.

"That's it," Fawn purred. "Let me see it, Arlon."

Her hand sped up, moving with purpose. In his ropes, his body went taut, mouth dropping open as his end rushed out of him. He let out a choked sound of pleasure, shuddering as he came over her hand. It seemed to last forever, and when it finally abated, he slumped into the hold of the ropes.

Fawn pressed a kiss to his sweaty forehead. "Well done, *a'marra.*"

He let out a breathless laugh as Fawn circled behind him and started to untie him. Once she freed his arms and legs, he spread out on the floor of her room, just enjoying the freedom.

Fawn settled on the rug beside him before she pulled the glowing focuses from around his fingers. She presented them to him and said, "Congratulations on conduiting for your first spell, Arlon. Though I'm curious to see what sort of spell we made."

He took the rings as the knot of emotion he'd carried through the spell tightened. He let out a long breath as he closed his eyes, holding the focuses against his chest.

Fawn's hand was gentle as she stroked through his hair. "How are you feeling?"

Arlon swallowed, his throat suddenly tight as an emotion he wasn't sure what to do with welled up inside of him. Bridgette's frank observation from the other night floated through his head.

Was this what love felt like?

It was a difficult realization to grapple with. For a time, he had thought he loved Vian, but the man had proved him so very wrong. He wasn't sure if he could trust the emotion that flooded him now.

Fawn drew him out of the troubling thoughts as she stroked his cheek. "Arlon?"

He let out a frustrated breath and said, "I don't understand why this is so hard for me. Because I-I *liked* that, I just..."

He trailed off, unsure how to finish that thought, but Fawn finished it for him. "You just have a hard time believing you're truly safe here."

His next exhale shuddered out of him as that truth sank in.

"You've been taught that letting your guard down will get you hurt," she said, her fingers stroking comfortingly through his hair. "That vulnerability will be punished, but to be an effective conduit, you *have* to allow yourself to be vulnerable."

Arlon let out a helpless sort of laugh as he moved to bury his face against her lap. As usual, she saw the reality of it all easier than he did. Knew him better than he knew himself. What was that if not love?

"Fuck."

"You're pushing yourself too hard. This was your first time. Once you have enough good experiences to eclipse the bad, I think you'll find conduiting... freeing."

"Maybe," Arlon said, though he hoped she was right. He knew what conspace looked like. Had shot Fawn into it a few times now, seen the perfect bliss on her face. And part of him wished to know what it was like to have every worry, every thought shut off. Magic would be so much easier to make without the weight of the heavy thoughts he was carrying.

Fawn leaned down to press a kiss against his cheek, and he could feel her smile against his skin. Her voice was barely above a whisper. "You look so beautiful on your knees, *a'marra.*"

That same indiscernible emotion welled in his chest. He felt full with it, fit to break.

"I think I'll always prefer casting," he murmured, "but... I'd kneel for you again."

8

The next morning, Arlon woke to the familiar rainbow shine of sunlight on magiline. He was spooned against Fawn's back, one arm slung over her waist, but she stirred as he pressed a kiss to her bare shoulder.

She rolled to face him, her black hair mussed. Her face was still creased with sleep, and he reached out to brush a stray strand from her cheek. She let out a contented sigh as she cuddled her pillow close.

Seeing her like this never got old, and he felt privileged to witness the woman behind the Grandmaster so intimately. He just hoped it was a privilege he wasn't abusing.

"Sorry," he murmured, breaking the comfortable quiet. "Didn't mean to fall asleep here."

Conduiting last night had drained him in a way he wasn't expecting. It felt like he'd given more than just magic to the new rings that adorned his slowly growing spell necklace. Any idea of going back to his own room had vanished the moment Fawn's fingers started dragging through his hair.

She cradled her cheek on one hand as she looked up at him. "You don't need to apologize."

Arlon frowned. It hadn't passed his attention that he seemed to be the lone wizard of the Crux that was allowed into the Grandmaster's quarters on a regular basis. "But why am I the only person who ever spends the night with you?"

The question seemed to chase away her lingering sleepiness. She considered him before she said, "It gets... complicated with this position. Sex is the nature of our work, but forming deeper relationships outside of casting and conduiting can be... detrimental for my wizards."

Unease prickled against his neck. "So what happens now that *I'm* one of your wizards?"

Fawn turned her eyes up to him. "You were my lover before you were one of my wizards."

"And I was your prisoner before I was your lover," he pointed out.

Fawn chuckled and said, "You have always been a conflict of interest."

That didn't help Arlon's unease. "I don't want to stop being your lover just to be one of your wizards."

Fawn scooted closer to him, one leg twining around his. "I'm not asking you to. You can be both, but as with everything we do inside of the Crux, there is a risk to it."

"What risk?"

"Being a wizard isn't just sex and magic, Arlon," she said. "We have a job, and a perilous one at that. We're protectors and servants of the realm, and there will inevitably come a time when I make a decision you disagree with or give you an order you don't like. But I am Grandmaster, and that means I will *always* have a disproportionate amount of power in our relationship—whatever form that relationship takes. I will always take council, but when I give an order, I have to trust that my wizards will obey, even if they disagree. Can you do that?"

Arlon studied her face, swallowing the knot of emotion that had formed in his throat. Maybe this really was what love felt like.

"I'd go to the ends of the world for you."

Fawn's smile took on a sad tilt. "I know. And that's what scares me about you."

Arlon's stomach dropped, and he couldn't help but think he'd done something... wrong. He didn't know what to say, so he said nothing, but Fawn could read his unease like a book.

"I felt your potential as a wizard the moment I laid a hand on you. I knew that I was creating a potentially complicated situation when I intervened to commute your sentence, *a'marra*." She rested a hand on his chest, her fingers brushing the edge of the crescent scar that peeked through the v of his shirt. "But what I didn't know at the time was how much I would come to care about you."

Arlon's chest filled with a painful sort of happiness at the declaration. But the part of him that expected anything good to be accompanied by something far worse asked, "Do you regret it?"

"Would it be less complicated if I hadn't fallen in love with you? Yes." Fawn smiled up at him and said, "But you are more than worth the risk."

The statement made Arlon's heart thud against his ribcage. Hearing it spoken so plainly helped him see the knotted web of her loyalties. Her duty to the Crown and the realm, her duty to her wizards and the Crux, the duty she owed herself and her own happiness.

You're also in love with her. I have eyes, you know.

Bridgette had said it like it was the most obvious thing in the world. So obvious that she'd seen it after one conversation.

So why did the realization blindside Arlon?

He suddenly saw how precarious of a position he'd fallen into with Fawn. A risk, indeed. One that was bound to get him hurt. Nothing good in his life ever lasted, and his relationship with Fawn would be no different.

Only heartache would come from falling in love with the Grandmaster of the Crux, yet he couldn't seem to help himself. He was drawn to her like a lodestone, and he helplessly followed the unspoken command. He shifted to kneel over her, burying his face against her neck as he closed his eyes. Her arms raised to circle his shoulders, one leg twining over his hip, and his body responded automatically.

The first time he ever laid eyes on her, Fawn had burst into the Wolves' camp, flames dancing over her spell-wrapped hands. She'd looked like a demon, her eyes dark with purpose, teeth bared in a snarl. In that moment, Arlon knew she would be the death of him. As he breathed in the scent of her juniper soap now, he was certain that was still true.

Which left only one road he could take to save himself. He pressed a kiss to her neck before he pulled away. He'd gotten far too close.

"I should go. I don't want to leave Garrett waiting."

Fawn hummed, stretching luxuriously as Arlon slid out of her bed. If she noticed the sudden change of topic, the lack of reciprocation to the war hammer of a declaration she'd just given him, she didn't press the issue. Something he was grateful for. He couldn't talk about it. Not now.

"Speaking of Garrett," Fawn said, "I have a surprise for you both today."

Arlon turned to look at her, eyebrow raised. "What surprise?"

Her smile was bright as she looked up at him. "Bring Garrett to my office later this morning, and I'll show you."

The promise of that surprise carried him through a bath and breakfast. When it was finally time to meet Garrett, the other man was already waiting for him in the evocation yard. At Arlon's news, he was eager to follow, and together they walked the short trip to Fawn's office at record speed.

As they opened the door, Fawn looked up with a grin. She got to her feet, seemingly as excited as they were. Then, she opened the door to the dungeon, and Arlon raised a skeptical eyebrow.

"It's downstairs?" he asked.

Fawn chuckled and said, "It was the only room big enough to house it."

Arlon shared a look with Garrett before he led the way down. Fawn followed behind them, touching one of the glow globes to chase the gloom from the dungeon. And as they brightened, Arlon found the new addition immediately.

A woven mat lay on the floor. It was tucked into the far end of the room, all stored casting equipment relocated elsewhere.

Garrett was too busy surveying the rest of the room to even notice it. He must not have seen the full might of the dungeon before, and his wide-eyed shock made Arlon grin and slap his chest before pointing to the mat.

"Oh," Garrett said with a bark of a laugh. "For a second, I didn't know what kind of surprise this was supposed to be."

Arlon thought he detected something like disappointment, but no. Garrett's smile was bright as he walked over to the mat. He threw himself down in a side fall, slapping the mat as he landed, and the satisfying *smack* echoed around the dungeon. An appreciative groan escaped him as he flopped onto his back, his hands sliding across the woven surface.

"Gods, that is so much better than dirt."

"I'm glad that it suits," Fawn said. "So long as the dungeon isn't in use, you two are welcome to come down any time."

Arlon stared at the mat, not sure how to feel. Fawn had surprised him many times, but not like this. So many of the gifts she had given him had been a necessity. But this was a gift given just because it would make them happy.

"Thank you," he said, the words rough with emotions he didn't know how to sort through.

Fawn beamed and leaned up to press a kiss to his lips. "You're welcome, *a'marra*."

"You can watch or join, if you have any interest, Grandmaster. I'm happy to teach anyone," Garrett called, and Arlon quickly turned away to wipe his eyes.

Fawn chuckled and said, "No, that's alright. I don't want to intrude." She pressed one more kiss to Arlon's cheek before she headed for the stairs. "I hope you enjoy it."

Arlon watched her go, his heart tied into a knot, but Garrett snapped him out of it as he slapped a hand against the mat again. The crack echoed off the walls, bringing Arlon crashing back into himself.

"Well, c'mon then," Garrett crowed, his smile bright. "Let's break it in."

9

From that day on, the dungeon replaced the evocation yard as their usual meeting spot. As summer arrived in earnest, the room remained blessedly cool. Not to mention, the privacy allowed Arlon to spar without the looming thought that someone might be watching his many, *many* failures.

But slowly, gradually, Garrett's lessons started to pay off.

Improvement came in fits and spurts. Arlon would catch Garrett off guard, squirm out of his hold. He even got close to pinning him a couple of times before the other man inevitably, *infuriatingly* managed to turn the tables.

"How the *fuck* do you do that?" Arlon panted after Garrett released him from an arm lock.

"I told you, you have to feel out your opponent," Garrett said as he popped back to his feet. He stretched his arms in front of him as he cast a toothy grin down at Arlon. "I can feel where you distribute your weight. Can feel when you're getting tired. When your grip loosens."

Arlon groaned and rolled to sit, stroking a hand through his sweat-soaked hair. "Doesn't explain how you manage to get me on my back."

Garrett offered him a hand up, chuckling. "That's just timing."

Arlon took it and let himself be pulled to his feet. "When do you learn that?"

Garrett just winked before he squared off again. "You keep losing until you find out."

When Arlon asked to increase the duration of their sparring sessions, Garrett was happy to agree. Arlon told himself that it was his drive to get better, but some small part of him recognized the true reason. The more time he spent with Garrett, the less time he could spend with Fawn.

If the Grandmaster noticed that Arlon had stopped taking his meals with her, chose to read in the library or outside rather than in her office, found reasons to leave soon after their casting lessons concluded, she hadn't said anything. Ever since he'd been granted his freedom, Arlon had clung to her like a fungus, so he couldn't help but wonder if Fawn was a little relieved by his absence now.

But the distance wasn't easy to maintain. Fawn was like a current he couldn't seem to escape. He craved the safety of her office, her room, but so many past experiences told him that he couldn't trust that feeling. He'd gotten too comfortable, too close.

He loved her, but that could never last. Creating distance now would only help when the invisible force connecting them finally snapped.

But without the safety of Fawn, he was forced out into the Crux, and lingering in the common areas made him feel like a mouse waiting to be snatched by an owl. The looks were ever present, but talk of how he'd treated Magda a few weeks ago must have spread. No one approached him, though that didn't stop him from constantly looking over his shoulder, tensing whenever someone made eye contact before they quickly, inevitably moved on.

The dungeon soon became the only place he could avoid the attention. So maybe that was why it came as such a shock when Bridgette followed Garrett down the stairs to the dungeon one morning. Arlon must have been bad at hiding his surprise, because Garrett's smile faded.

"Bridgette was curious to see where we've been practicing, so I thought she could watch today," Garrett said. "I'm sorry, I should have asked first."

"If you're not alright with it, I can go," Bridgette said before she stood up on her toes to press a kiss against her husband's cheek. "Have fun."

"No, no, it's fine," Arlon said quickly. "You just surprised me is all."

Bridgette hummed, amusement quirking the corner of her lips. "Turnabout's fair play, then."

Arlon couldn't help but chuckle, remembering how he'd scared the shit out of her when he'd burst from his room a few weeks ago. "You should stay."

This was the first time he'd really seen her since that night, and he was grateful to have another opportunity. It felt like they'd come to an understanding of one another while smoking in the transmutation yard. She had more reason to fear him than anyone in the Crux, so the fact that she was here now felt significant.

Bridgette grinned before she took a seat on a padded spanking bench, seemingly at ease among all of the casting equipment. "Alright. I'll be happy to watch my husband put you on the ground again."

There was a hint of a challenge in her voice that stoked the fires of Arlon's competitiveness. "Bold assumption."

Bridgette's grin was full of mischief. "From what Garrett's been telling me about your little basement sparring sessions, it is not."

Any other time, Arlon might have gotten defensive, but the jab was good-natured on top of being true. He chuckled and said, "Maybe with you here, I'll get lucky."

Bridgette's blue eyes looked him over, appraising. Her smile turned sly. "Bet you could, big boy."

It took Arlon a moment longer to realize that she might not be talking about sparring anymore. The comment should have made him uncomfortable, but hearing it from her shot a pulse of unexpected warmth through him.

Garrett let out a bark of a laugh. "Maybe having you come down to watch was a mistake. You're going to be a distraction, aren't you?"

Bridgette hummed as she twirled one silver strand of hair coyly around her finger. "Only as much of a distraction as you two want. Topless cheering squad is on the table."

Garrett laughed, and Arlon couldn't help but echo it even as his neck flushed hot. But now that she'd said it, he couldn't help but imagine it. There was no denying she was beautiful, even fully clothed.

"Is that a yes?" Bridgette teased as she reached for the laces of her dress.

"You are a menace," Garrett said as he stripped off his shirt and tossed it aside.

"That still isn't an answer," she countered, her grin widening. "What do you think, Arlon? I'll keep him distracted, and you can pin him."

Arlon's face felt hot enough to catch fire, but he laughed all the same. It was a tempting offer on a few different fronts, but one he couldn't accept. "No way. If I'm going to beat him, I'm going to do it distraction-free."

Bridgette winked at him before she released her laces and leaned back against the spanking bench. "Suit yourself. Let's see you take him down, big boy."

Chuckling, Arlon gave her a mock bow before he went to join Garrett on the mat. The other man's cheeks were flushed a few shades darker, though he couldn't seem to wipe the grin from his face.

"For fuck's sake, are you stretched out or not?" Garrett asked as he lifted loose fists.

Arlon rolled his neck out. "I'm ready."

They squared off, and it was only then Arlon realized he'd gotten used to reading Garrett. Because with Bridgette here, the feel of him, his energy, suddenly *changed*.

It was like a fire had been lit. Garrett's smile was no less genuine, but the light in his eye told Arlon that this wasn't going to be an easy spar. Garrett was playing to win, and Arlon braced himself for the challenge.

Garrett called the start of the match in his native tongue before Arlon lunged. He swung a kick towards his thigh, but Garrett blocked and countered. A fist connected with Arlon's ribs, reminding him to keep his godsdamned elbows down, which he did just in time to stop a second strike. Arlon kept his guard up, searching for an opening.

Garrett found it first as he turned in, twisting his legs through Arlon's as he went for a throw. Arlon managed to step out of it—barely. The failed attempt put Garrett off-balance, and Arlon pressed his advantage as he lunged forward, arms wrapping around Garrett's waist. His leg twined between Garrett's, going for a trip only to stumble as the other man stepped deftly out of it.

Garrett's arms wrapped around his torso, locking them

together as they vied for the upper hand. The proximity helped him feel every shift of Garrett's feet, every time he tensed his core or adjusted his grip. Arlon kept his own legs wide, holding a strong stance to avoid getting his feet knocked out from under him with a lucky swipe.

It was a stalemate until, between breaths, Arlon felt an opening. He surged forward with all of his strength, bringing his leg up just in time to trip Garrett over it. The other man went down, eyes flying wide, and it was only that surprise that allowed Arlon to get on him. He grabbed Garrett's leg, twining around it like a snake before he flipped the other man onto his front, twisting his leg into a lock.

There was a sharp tap against the mat. Arlon was so surprised that it took him a second longer to loosen his grip. Garrett rolled onto his back before letting out a booming laugh. They were still entangled on the mat, but Garrett gave him a good-natured shove as he crowed, "*That's* what I'm talking about!"

Arlon let out a hesitant chuckle, still in shock that he'd actually won. He detangled his sweaty legs from around Garrett's and fell back onto the mat to catch his breath. Bridgette came into focus above him, a towel in hand. He took it gratefully, wiping the sweat from his face.

"Not bad, Arlon. You've definitely learned some tricks since the last time," Bridgette said approvingly.

"Gods, I'd hope so," Arlon panted, too tired to sit up. "All it took was months of getting my ass kicked."

"Yeah, well, ass-kicking is the first step to learning," Garrett laughed breathlessly, his smile bright. "Well done, Arlon."

"Was this the first time you beat him?" Bridgette asked, and when Arlon nodded, her grin widened. "I'm glad I got to see it. Garrett could use a good beating every now and again."

"Hey now, you were supposed to be *my* good luck charm today," Garrett huffed.

Bridgette hummed, her eyes twinkling with amusement. "Guess you'll have to share, love."

Arlon couldn't quite decipher the twin looks that flashed his direction. All he knew was that he left the dungeon feeling lighter than air.

10

Summer crept on, and as the weeks passed, the heat outside drove Bridgette down into the dungeon with Arlon and Garrett more and more often. Her company was welcome, and not just because she was happy to refill their water jugs or fetch towels when they sweated through their clothes. Her presence changed the whole tone of their sparring matches from strenuous lessons to something far more fun.

"C'mon Arlon, you let him have that one!"

Arlon chuckled breathlessly as he lay sprawled on the mat, trying to cool off after the most recent bout. "You want to try and do better?"

Bridgette grinned as she tossed a towel onto his face. "I would, but Garrett doesn't like how I spar."

"That's because your version of 'sparring' usually involves putting a finger in me," Garrett snorted. "And we're fighting down here, not fucking."

"Shame," Bridgette tsked. "Don't get me wrong, I like watching you two spar, but it would be far more exciting if more fingers went into Garrett."

85

Arlon laughed as he rolled onto his front to give his back a chance to cool off. And if it had the added bonus of hiding how his cock had perked up at that idea, he kept that to himself.

Between the three of them, they fell into an easy routine. They'd wake up, get breakfast in the mess hall, and head down to the dungeon together. But that routine was interrupted when they arrived at Fawn's office one morning and found the door locked.

"Oh, hell," Arlon muttered. "I forgot Fawn said she would be using the dungeon today."

"For what?"

"It's for—uh." Arlon paused, wracking his memory for the Maeve wizard's name. "Ivarrian's mastery petition. I think they're going for transmutation."

Garrett's lips quirked into a grin. "Good for them."

"So long as Fawn leaves them in one piece, that is," Bridgette pointed out.

Garrett chuckled. "Less good for us."

Arlon rubbed his neck. "We could always go back to the evocation yard?"

Garrett made a face at that as Bridgette said, "What if I had a better idea?"

"Yeah?" Arlon asked.

"Dmitry invited me to go into town today with Edrei and Magda, but I turned him down," Bridgette said. "Since the dungeon's occupied, why don't we go join them?"

Arlon crossed his arms over his chest, falling quiet. Beside him, Garrett sighed and said, "I don't know, Bri. After last night, I was sort of hoping for... less people."

Bridgette tsked before she turned to Arlon. "What about you?"

Arlon blinked. "What about me?"

She rolled her eyes before saying, "Do you want to come?"

For some reason, the idea that Bridgette might want him to join without Garrett there surprised him. Maybe that's why he fumbled out an uncertain, "I—yeah, I guess."

Bridgette beamed at him, and the sight made heat creep up his neck. "Then go get changed. I'll make sure they haven't left yet. We'll wait for you out in the courtyard."

She hurried off down the hall, and all at once, Arlon realized what he'd agreed to.

"You alright?" Garrett asked.

Arlon's hands had suddenly gone clammy. "I don't..."

Garrett looked him over. He seemed to read Arlon's unease just as easily as he read his movements on the sparring mat. "Is it the going into town part or the going with others part that's freaking you out?"

The frankness of the question made him straighten. His voice emerged tight and clipped. "I'm not freaked out."

Garrett gave him an unamused look. "Arlon."

He blinked. There was no real threat, but he'd gone on the defensive without thought. He forced out an annoyed breath. "Both?"

Garrett hummed as he pushed away from the wall. "What if I came with?"

Arlon scowled. "You said you wanted less people."

"When I said 'less people,' I meant I was hoping to just spend the day with you and Bri," Garrett chuckled.

Something warm pooled in Arlon's chest at that declaration. It helped soothe the knot of his uncertainty. "Oh."

"So, what do you say? I'll go if you do."

Any other time, Arlon would have tapped out, but Garrett was a fortifying presence. Besides, spending time with him and Bridgette was the only thing Arlon wanted out of today, too.

"Alright," Arlon said before he could talk himself out of it. "Let's go."

They hurried up to their rooms to change into something more substantial than sparring clothes before they went to the courtyard. Bridgette was there to meet them, though she had donned a sun hat to go with the airy summer dress she wore. With her was a small group of three wizards that Arlon knew by face, if not by name.

A Kenitkan man with a strong jaw stood beside Magda and Bridgette, his smile bright against his dark brown skin. They were talking to a willowy Lenear man, but as Arlon and Garrett approached, all eyes turned to look their way. It made Arlon's skin prickle, and he followed a half step behind Garrett as they approached.

Bridgette raised an eyebrow at her husband, but Garrett just grinned. "Changed my mind."

Bridgette hummed, amusement tilting her lips. "Arlon, this is Edrei, Magda, and Dmitry."

"We've met," Magda said with a smile. "It's good to see you again, Arlon."

"Likewise," Arlon said. After the cold reception he had given her the last time they talked, he assumed the woman wouldn't want anything more to do with him.

"I'm glad Bridgette finally lured the recluse out," Dmitry said before he swept forward to offer a hand. "It's good to officially meet you, Arlon."

Arlon wasn't sure he liked being thrust into the middle of such attention, but after only a moment's hesitation, he took the Lenear man's hand. His head barely reached Arlon's shoulder, and his hand felt so delicate that Arlon was afraid he'd break it. Yet when Dmitry turned that bright smile up at him, Arlon was struck by how beautiful the man was. Golden-brown hair curled around his ears, matching his skin that seemed to glow like shined copper.

"Dmitry's been dying for an introduction," Bridgette teased.

Dmitry's pretty face flushed dark, and his smile turned sheepish. "When the handsome staff member starts wrestling Garrett in the evocation yard, it's hard not to take notice." He cleared his throat as he released Arlon's hand. "Like I said, it's good to officially meet you."

Arlon blinked down at the slender man in surprise and didn't know what else to say but, "Good to meet you, too."

Edrei put a hand on Magda's shoulder and said, "Are we ready?"

"Let's go," Bridgette said and led the way out of the courtyard, twining her arm around Dmitry's.

Garrett nudged Arlon's ribs before nodding towards Dmitry. "I think you've got an admirer."

Arlon gave a noncommittal grunt, but as they headed down the road towards town, he noticed Dmitry cast a few glances back his way. When Arlon caught his gaze during one such look, Dmitry's eyes went wide, his cheeks flushing before he quickly turned away.

Arlon's lips quirked into a grin. Garrett's hunch didn't appear to be wrong, and it was a bit of a thrill to realize he could fluster the man with little more than a look.

"How are you feeling after last night, Garrett?" Edrei asked, pulling Arlon from his thoughts.

"You should be asking Bridgette, not me," Garrett chuckled.

Edrei's grin turned sly as he and Magda fell into step beside them. "We heard plenty of how Bridgette felt about it. Just wondered how it was to watch."

Garrett smirked and said, "Whenever Bri's having a good

time, I'm having a good time. And you two *definitely* showed her a good time."

Edrei laughed as Magda said, "If you ever want in on the fun, all you have to do is say the word."

Garrett's cheeks flushed dark, his grin crooked. "I know it. Maybe someday."

It was no secret that Garrett often watched when Bridgette cast or conduited with others, but as Arlon stared resolutely at the back of Bridgette's head, he imagined himself in Edrei's or Magda's place. His loose trousers hid how much his cock took interest in the idea, but he was so lost in the thought that he didn't realize Magda had come to walk beside him until she slid her arm through his. The sudden, unexpected touch jolted him out of his fantasy.

"I've been meaning to talk to you," she said, and there was an uncertainty in her voice that surprised Arlon. "I wanted to apologize."

Of all the things Arlon had expected her to say, that was not it. "For what?"

"For coming onto you so strongly," she said with a wry grin. "I was afraid I'd scared you off the last time we talked."

"Oh," Arlon said, surprised for a second time.

"I'm used to dealing with other bloodline wizards," she admitted. "Being forward with our interest is... routine for us, but talking to Bridgette and Garrett has opened my eyes a bit to how jarring the Crux must be for someone who's new to magic."

Arlon couldn't help a small laugh, though hearing her address it made it feel like an invisible weight had just lifted. "Jarring is one way to put it."

"And how would you put it?" Magda asked.

Arlon clicked his teeth, remembering the hungry look she'd first given him. "It feels like being prey."

Magda winced as her arm tightened around his. The longer she held onto him, the more he found that he enjoyed the warmth of the innocent touch.

"I'm sorry if I contributed to that feeling," she said sincerely. "That wasn't my intention."

Arlon glanced down at her curiously. He'd always felt a rift between him and the greater population of the Crux, but this seemed like a chance to bridge it. "Let's clear the air, then. What was your intention?"

Magda chuckled, brushing one twisted coil of hair behind her ear. "To let you know that I think you're very handsome? And I'm curious to know more about you. Inside and outside of a casting room."

The answer surprised him with its simplicity, and all at once, Arlon realized exactly what the rift he'd felt was. It wasn't due to the disparity of his station or the shadow of his past. It was his willingness to let other people get close.

Arlon's walls still stood, but it felt like his time at the Crux had loosened the mortar holding them all together. It left him feeling a little unsteady, a little off-balance with the realization that... it was just that easy, wasn't it?

Dmitry's voice pulled him from his thoughts as the man called out, "Jot me down as also curious."

"And by 'curious,' they mean they'll ride you like the fastest horse in the stables if you let them," Bridgette said.

Arlon couldn't stop a bark of a laugh, his face flushing hot. "Fucking wizards," he muttered even as the thought of Garrett and Bridgette floated back into his head. "I'll think about it."

II

Arlon's arm was locked tight around Garrett's neck, legs hooked around his thighs in an iron grip. Every muscle screamed as Garrett fought against his hold, scooting them across the mat with the force of his struggles. Then, Garrett tapped his arm, and Arlon released him with a ragged shout of triumph.

For a second, neither of them moved, and Arlon was too tired to care that his legs were still hooked around Garrett's. Finally, the other man stirred, rolling flat onto his stomach as he sprawled out on the mat.

"Fuck me, but you're strong for a human."

Arlon took a second to gather his own breath before he said, "Might not be all human. Might be part Tariten, but hell if I know."

Above him, Bridgette stepped into his field of view, her finger hooked around the handle of a water jug. Arlon groaned, his core muscles screaming at him as he sat up to take it with a word of thanks.

"You know, that was the first thing Dmitry asked me about

you?" Bridgette said as she offered a second water jug to her husband. "He thought you might be Tariten due to your size."

Arlon snorted but finished a few long gulps before he wiped his mouth. "He's never met a full Tariten, then. Even the smallest have at least three heads on me." He took another long drink before saying, "But you can tell Dmitry my cock is proportional to the rest of me. I know he's wondering."

Bridgette's laugh was bright. "He will be thrilled to hear it. Though he'd like it more if you showed it to him."

Arlon grinned over the mouth of the jug. "I'll bet he would."

Ever since his conversation with Magda on the road into town, Arlon felt like he had a better understanding of the other wizards of the Crux. Sex was a casual sort of thing here, just like it had been among Vian's Wolves. But unlike the Wolves, the fact that sex was a part of the job felt like a safeguard against being stabbed in the back if he allowed himself to get close. And since his relationship with Fawn had devolved into complicated, messy emotions, the idea of sex with no strings attached was growing more tempting by the day.

Arlon took another sip from the water jug only to catch Garrett's eyes tracing him through the fabric of his shorts. Yet as Arlon lowered the jug, Garrett's eyes snapped away before the man asked, "You up for another round?"

Arlon smirked, trying to ignore the heat that had crept up his neck. "Depends. You looking to get beat again?"

Garrett laughed even as that competitive glint lit in his eye. "It was a lucky maneuver. Caught me by surprise, is all."

"I don't know, love. I think you've created a monster by training him," Bridgette said.

Garrett swallowed a mouthful of water before he met his wife's eyes. "You know, wasn't until you started coming down to watch that I started losing."

"Do I make you nervous?" she teased.

Garrett hummed, his gray eyes smoldering. "In all the best ways."

Bridgette's smile was bright. "Well, if I'm such a distraction, why don't I just leave?"

"But then you'd miss out on me pinning Garrett again," Arlon said as he nudged Garrett in the ribs.

Garrett groaned. "Gods, I *have* created a monster."

Bridgette hummed, her eyes twinkling with amusement as she looked between the two of them. "Is that a promise, Arlon? Never thought I'd enjoy the sight of my husband getting pinned by another man quite so much."

The sultry wink Bridgette aimed at Arlon made his heart forget its job for a hot second. He took another long drink to avoid trying to find a response.

"As often as you cuck me, it seems like you're itching to be the one in the chair," Garrett teased. He set the water jug aside and leaned back on his elbows, spreading his legs out on the mat to cool off.

Over the lip of the water jug, Arlon couldn't help but sneak a look. Unlike him, Garrett always sparred without a shirt, and the airy shorts he wore left little to the imagination. From how close they got while sparring, Arlon knew that he wasn't the only one with... good proportions.

Bridgette chuckled as she walked across the mat to her husband, her airy summer dress flowing as she planted one sandaled foot on his chest. With a stern shove, she pushed him flat, pinning him under her foot. Her voice adopted an edge of warning as she asked, "What'd you just say?"

Garrett bit his bottom lip, his gray eyes turned to thunderclouds. "You heard me."

The energy seemed to crackle between the two of them, like a spell waiting to be cast. It made the hair on Arlon's neck stand to attention, his mouth suddenly dry as he watched them out of the corner of his eye. Bridgette considered her husband before she finally lifted her foot.

"You know, Arlon," Bridgette said, and something in her voice shot straight to his groin, "I wouldn't mind watching one more round." She looked at him with eyes that burned like coals. "And if you pin him again, you can fuck him if you want."

Arlon's heart leapt into his throat, cutting off his response. She winked as she retreated to her seat along the wall, and Garrett chuckled as he sat up, rubbing his chest. Arlon fully expected him to laugh the suggestion off, yet when Garrett looked at him, desire was written plainly on his flushed face.

"I mean... I'm alright with that," Garrett said, and the quiet hope in his voice rang in Arlon's ears like a bell.

Suddenly, Arlon had to reassess every moment he'd spent with the other man. The times he caught Garrett looking when they were in the baths, the brush of a half-hard cock during a grapple that he had sworn he'd imagined. It all dawned on him like a slap to the face.

Garrett *wanted* him. And going off the look on Bridgette's face, maybe she did, too.

Arlon froze like a mouse caught in a corner. He didn't know what to say, what to do as his heart raced faster than it ever had during a spar. With the two of them looking at him, waiting for his answer, he felt like he was teetering on a knife's edge of fear and desire.

Because he wanted them back. And being faced with the reality of that terrified him for reasons he couldn't put his finger on.

"I'm sorry, that was a stupid suggestion," Bridgette said, taking his silence for a refusal. Yet the disappointment in her voice jolted Arlon out of his own spiraling thoughts.

"No, no. It's not," he said before he cleared the nervous

tremble from his throat. He looked at Garrett as he asked, "But what would happen if *you* win?"

Garrett seemed to read the fear on his face. "Whatever you want to happen."

Arlon's tongue darted out to wet his suddenly dry lips. His mind raced as he tried to decide *what* he was alright with, but trying to process all of that at once overwhelmed him. His thoughts spiraled into a panic that was only broken when a gentle finger tapped the underside of his chin. It jolted him out of it so abruptly, he gasped as he lifted his head to meet Garrett's kind smile.

"Hey, relax," the other man said gently. "Let's just spar, yeah? Then we can decide what we want to do after."

Arlon grasped onto the familiar as he nodded. "Yeah. Yeah, let's do that."

Garrett smiled as he stood before offering Arlon a hand up. He took it, allowing himself to be pulled to his feet. All the while, he could feel Bridgette watching them, her gaze hot as a flame.

"Ready?" Garrett asked as he sank into a strong stance.

Arlon breathed a swear, shaking out his trembling hands before he lifted his fists. "Ready."

"*Ekat!*" Garrett barked before lunging forward. Arlon sidestepped the grab and countered with a punch to the ribs. It didn't quite get through the other man's guard, but Garrett grunted at the impact all the same. Arlon's knee quickly followed, and Garrett took a staggering step back.

"Good job making that opening," Garrett panted before he lunged again, going lower. Arlon wasn't quite able to step out of the way, but he widened his stance to just barely avoid being toppled. Garrett's head was tucked against his stomach, arms held strong around his waist, and Arlon locked his grip around Garrett's torso.

No matter which way Garrett moved, Arlon countered, keeping his legs well out of tripping distance. When Garrett shoved, Arlon shoved back, doggedly keeping his balance even as his strength started to falter. He'd gone all out in the last match and sweat made his grip start to slip.

In the split second it took to readjust it, Garrett found his opening. The other man threw his weight forward with a roar, breaking Arlon's grip as he tackled him around the middle. It sent them both to the ground, but Arlon wasn't down and out yet.

He thrust his hips up with all of his might, trying to dislodge Garrett. And for a second, he thought it worked. The other man's weight lifted, yet when Arlon tried to scramble out from under him, regain his feet, Garrett tripped him onto his front. Weight bore down on him, pinning his cheek and shoulders against the mat as a gray forearm snaked around his neck, choking off his air. Arlon knew it was over, but he struggled until his vision started to darken at the edges before he finally tapped.

The arm around his neck loosened, and Arlon dragged in a grateful breath. Garrett lifted his weight a little, his arms moving to plant on either side of his head. Yet he didn't get off of him like he usually did.

Instead, one knee settled between Arlon's legs. Hot breath tickled at his ear. It made Arlon shiver as fear and desire collided in him.

"Is this alright?" Garrett asked, his voice a low, breathless rumble.

Even though Garrett had touched Arlon hundreds of times during their spars, it had never been like this. The energy between them had changed, shifted between breaths from sport to something else. Yet that part of him that wanted to flee quieted at the question. He could tap out at any time.

"Yes."

Garrett's head lowered, his breath turning to a gale by Arlon's ear. Tusks and lips brushed against the back of his neck before a tongue darted out to taste the sweat on his skin. "And this?"

Arlon shuddered. The warmth of his breath made the skin on his neck ripple, every hair standing on edge. Fear tugged at the darkest parts of his memories, but once again, the quiet rumble of Garrett's question staved it off.

"Yes."

"Good," Garrett murmured before his teeth bit down gently. Arlon arched, spikes of pain radiating from where the tips of Garrett's tusks poked his skin. The residual rush from their spar was transformed to desire, surging hot. Arlon groaned, hands clenching to fists against the mat.

Yet unlike their spars, Garrett moved slow. He soothed the reddened spot on Arlon's neck with another gentle lick before he sat up. His knees settled between Arlon's legs before he spread them in one slow, smooth motion.

Arlon's first instinct was to fight the move, close himself off, but he forced the instinct back. It felt too exposed, vulnerable, even while wearing shorts and a shirt. But then Garrett's rough, calloused hand stroked gently down his back before a finger dipped at the edge of Arlon's shorts.

"Is this alright?" Garrett asked.

Arlon's heated skin felt electric under that gentle touch. "Yes."

Garrett's hand dipped further under his shorts, grazing over the muscles of his ass before coming to rest on his hip. He scooted his weight back, guiding Arlon up onto his hands and knees as that hand moved forward, tracing lines of fire across his hip. Fingers just barely brushed his cock through the airy shorts, but Arlon moaned all the same.

A smile crept into Garrett's voice as he asked, "And this?"

Arlon swore, his tired arms shaking as he held himself up. "F-fuck, yes."

Garrett's calloused hand wrapped around Arlon's straining length, making his hips buck entirely without his permission. His familiar weight settled against Arlon's back as his other hand slid under his shirt, coming up to tease at his chest. Rough fingers trailed through his chest hair until Garrett found a nipple and pinched gently.

Arlon shuddered as he rested his forehead against his forearm, eyes clenched shut as he panted for breath. The hand around his cock started to move, stroking gently, but the rough fingers felt so different from what he was used to with Fawn. A sharper sort of pleasure that wrung an appreciative hiss from his throat.

Garrett shifted behind him, though his hand stayed firmly wrapped around his cock. The hand on his chest slid down and back, moving to fill the scant space between them. His hand trailed over the swell of Arlon's ass before dipping down further, the thin shorts the only thing keeping him from touching his hole.

"And what about this?" Garrett asked.

Arlon sucked in a breath, pleasure racing through him at the touch. The hand on his cock paused, allowing him enough of his wits back to think. Fear chased him like a shadow, but Garrett was patient as he waited for his answer.

"I-I'll try," Arlon said at last.

Garrett hummed as if hearing all of the things that Arlon didn't want to say in those two words. Like he could read his fear and hurt from the only other time a man had been inside of him. Gently, Garrett hooked his thumbs over the hem of Arlon's shorts, before he pushed them down, exposing his ass and cock to the cool dungeon air.

"The second you tap, I stop," Garrett murmured. "No questions, alright?"

"Right," Arlon breathed before he lifted his head from his forearms to see Bridgette rise from her chair. The hem of her dress brushed the ground as she approached them, and she knelt on the mat in front of Arlon. She passed a little bottle of lube to Garrett before she cupped Arlon's cheek.

Arlon trembled under the gentle touch, his mouth suddenly dry as he looked up at her. Her silver hair made her look ethereal, unreal in the dim glow of the dungeon. Where Fawn was made of shadow, Bridgette seemed to be made of starlight, cold and bright. But there was a warmth in her eyes as she looked at him with an understanding that spoke volumes.

"Can I kiss you?" she asked.

The answer came as easy as breathing. "Yes."

She lifted his chin, tilting his head up before her lips pressed against his, soft as velvet. It sent a jolt of pleasure through him that was only echoed as Garrett's oiled finger teased at his entrance.

Arlon's eyes slid closed. Between the two of them, his walls dropped just as his lips parted.

Bridgette deepened the kiss, her tongue darting in to taste him as Garrett's thick finger eased deeper. Where Arlon expected to feel an echo of pain, he only felt a gentle stretch and an explosion of sensation. It made his head swim, and his moan was swallowed by Bridgette. Garrett's arm hooked around Arlon's chest, pulling him to kneel up.

Bridgette guided Arlon's arms around her shoulders, and he clung to her as Garrett pressed against his back. The change in position helped the other man's finger slide even deeper. His free hand trailed down Arlon's chest and stomach to grab his length again.

Time seemed to stop between the two of them. Bridgette nibbled his lower lip as her hand came down to join her husband's. The contrast of Garrett's big, rough palm wrapped around his shaft to Bridgette's soft, delicate fingers teasing his tip made him feel like he was going to come apart. And only then did Garrett slide a second finger into him.

Arlon broke the kiss, throwing his head back with a grunt as his eyes went wide. The stretch of Garrett's thick fingers bordered on uncomfortable, but it became an afterthought as he stroked over his prostate, making his already aching cock throb.

"Is that alright?" Garrett asked as he thrust gently, easing his fingers in deeper with every stroke.

"Yes," Arlon gasped. "*Yes.*"

Bridgette cupped the back of his head, pulling him down to meet her lips once again. He moaned into the kiss even as he returned it, matching her intensity until their teeth clacked together. His hands stroked down her sides, feeling the curve of her waist, the swell of her ass. He explored her with his hands, mapping out the shape of her even as he used her to stay grounded. And as Garrett thrust his fingers deep, she was there to swallow his quiet, guttural sound of pleasure.

When she finally pulled back, Arlon sucked in a grateful breath. Yet when she released his cock, he couldn't stop a quiet sound of disappointment. Bridgette grinned as she cupped his face with both hands, her thumb stroking gently over his lip.

Garrett's fingers scissored inside of him, wringing a gasp from him as he was stretched gently. His hips jerked, yet no matter how much he squirmed, Bridgette didn't release him. Instead, she traced the bow of his lip as she watched him intently. Like she enjoyed seeing the pleasured flush on his cheeks, the way his eyes widened, pupils dilated. And for once, after a lifetime of being stared at, Arlon was glad to be seen.

He nuzzled her hand as he gripped her waist, turning to kiss her fingers as Garrett continued to thrust and twist, his other hand working Arlon's cock until it leaked. It was so unlike what he was used to, felt better than he thought possible, but it just *wasn't enough.*

But Bridgette seemed to read the desperation on his face. She kissed him gently before murmuring, "I want to watch Garrett fuck you. And then *I* want to fuck you. Are you alright with that?"

"*Please,*" Arlon begged as his cock twitched in Garrett's grip. Behind him, the other man chuckled as his fingers slowly withdrew. It left Arlon feeling empty, his nerves alight with sensation.

Garrett's hand released his cock before it teased at the hem of Arlon's shirt. "Can I take your clothes off?" he asked, his voice a low rumble.

Arlon opened his mouth to answer, but he couldn't quite form the words. His clothes were his last bit of protection in this new, uncharted territory. But then fabric brushed his arms, and he watched Bridgette shed her dress. She shed her underthings next, tossing them aside as if being naked was as natural as breathing to her.

Yet it was the smile she leveled at him that helped Arlon find the courage to tug his shirt off. Garrett helped him with his shorts, pulling them from around his knees and tossing them aside. It helped level the playing field. Helped Arlon push aside his own self-consciousness.

Bridgette sat down on the mat in front of him, her hands gentle as she cupped his face again. Garrett's warm hands rested on his hips before they slid down, grabbing his ass before spreading gently. Arlon let out a quiet sound of need even as a fresh wave of fear raced up his back.

With how closely she watched him, Bridgette saw it. Her

face was full of understanding as she asked, "Are you sure this is alright? We can stop if you don't want this."

Arlon's words froze in his throat before Garrett brushed a gentle kiss against the small of his back. They handled him carefully, like he might break at any second. And he *did* feel fragile. As if now, with his walls toppled, he was one wrong move away from shattering between them.

It was a leap of faith to say, "It's alright."

Garrett's lips trailed up his spine before the head of his slicked cock came to press at Arlon's entrance. Arlon shuddered, tensing automatically before Bridgette drew him into a gentle kiss. Her fingers stroked through his hair, their breath mingling like she was breathing courage into him.

Arlon moaned against her lips before his muscles relaxed as he surrendered to them. Garrett's hands tightened on his waist before he slowly, carefully eased into him. The stretch was more than he expected, and Arlon's breath left him in a rush. His arms trembled, but Bridgette was there to support him, her lips smiling against his.

"He's thick, isn't he?" she purred, and Arlon wordlessly nodded. "You're taking him so well."

The praise washed over him like a warm breeze, sending gooseflesh skittering over his skin as Garrett gave a slow, shallow thrust. Arlon let out a low moan as Bridgette kissed down his jaw. Her voice was a breathy whisper by his ear. "That's it, big boy." Her soft hand reached down to wrap around Arlon's dripping length. "Let me hear you."

"F-fuck," Arlon gasped, skin rippling as Garrett's hips came to rest against his ass, his cock sheathed fully inside of him.

"Still alright?" Garrett asked, his own voice breathless with desire.

Arlon's head swam, lost in the high of pleasure. "Do you feel me tapping?"

Bridgette smirked against his neck before her teeth nipped gently. The spark of pain made Arlon's cock twitch in her grip.

"Sure don't," Garrett chuckled before he inched out, pulling back to the tip. "But I do want to hear you shout."

Garrett's hips snapped forward in one smooth motion, and Arlon's breath left him in a guttural groan. Bridgette's hand sped up around his cock, and Arlon quivered helplessly, torn between trying to thrust into her grip even as Garrett fucked into him again. It was a little rougher, a little deeper, and Arlon did shout then, his eyes flying wide as pleasure sparked through his body.

Arlon became aware of every way they were connected. From Bridgette's hand on his cock, her body so close to him that he could smell the scent of cloves and apple blossom clinging to her, to Garrett's hard length inside of him, his strong grip on his waist.

Arlon's mind went blank between the two of them, all fear and doubt erased by their touch and mutual pleasure. He rode the waves of sensation that seemed to ebb and flow with every thrust, every stroke. A vague part of him realized he wouldn't be able to finish like this, but he couldn't bring himself to care. The connection, the closeness, was somehow far more satisfying than his own pleasure.

Garrett's pace sped up, and Arlon savored the feel of opening around him again and again. All the while, Bridgette's hand never stopped as she murmured quiet praise and filth into his ear. "How does he feel, Arlon?"

Something like a whimper broke past his lips, a sound so out of place that he didn't even recognize himself. "G-good," he gasped. "*Fuck*, he feels good."

Bridgette chuckled as one hand slid through his hair before gripping hard. Arlon let out a shout of surprise as she pulled his head up, snapping him to attention. Her blue eyes were like the hottest part of a flame, alight with lust.

"Keep your eyes on me, big boy," she said as she let his rigid cock fall from her grip. "I want to see your face when he finishes in you."

Arlon felt like he was floating out of his body, his gaze drawn to her like a lodestone. He didn't think he could look away even if he wanted to. Behind him, Garrett's pace reached a fever pitch, his hips slapping against Arlon's ass with each deep thrust. One arm snaked around Arlon's chest before Garrett pulled him to kneel up, his pace never faltering.

The angle change made Arlon grunt, pulse roaring as Garrett's thrusts got rougher, more desperate. Tusks bit down on his shoulder, and Arlon shouted as his hand flew back to cup the other man's head. His hard cock bobbed with every jerk of Garrett's hips, his tip red and leaking. As much as he wanted to feel her grip around him again, Bridgette's hand had found something else to do.

Arlon could only watch as Bridgette leaned back and spread her knees before her hand slid down between her legs. She teased through pale curls until she reached the folds of her cunt and pressed one finger in. Arlon's length throbbed, a whimper of need escaping him as Garrett let out a low groan. The other man tensed, and with how they were connected, Arlon could feel the way Garrett's cock swelled before his end overtook him.

Garrett's hips stuttered to a stop, and Arlon let out a gasp as the other man's seed spilled into him. Arlon quivered as lips pressed gently against the back of his shoulder, Garrett's breath puffing against his skin. It was both a relief and a disappointment when Garrett pulled out of him, and Arlon couldn't help the full-bodied shudder that wracked him at the loss.

His vision swam into focus on Bridgette's flushed face. Her lower lip was held between her teeth, two fingers buried deep in her cunt. The sight made Arlon's hard cock bob, his need surging hot.

"Fuck," Bridgette whispered, her voice shaky with desire. "I don't think I could get tired of watching that."

"Told you. Cuckquean," Garrett chuckled before he pressed one more kiss to Arlon's shoulder. When he gently pushed him forward, Arlon fell onto his hands and knees in front of her. "Your turn."

Bridgette smiled as she pulled her fingers from her cunt to beckon Arlon closer. "Come on then, big boy."

He crawled forward in a daze, closing the distance between them. Some of Garrett's ample seed slid down his thigh, and Arlon shuddered as he wrapped his lips around Bridgette's fingers. Her lips parted in silent, delighted surprise as Arlon sucked her clean.

Once he was finished, Bridgette wrapped her arms around him, drawing his head down to her chest. Arlon obeyed the silent order as he found one pink nipple and pulled it into his mouth. Bridgette let out a breathy moan, her fingers gripped tight in his hair. Arlon kissed across her pale chest, tongue darting out to taste her skin.

Bridgette squirmed, quiet sounds of pleasure escaping her until she put a hand against his chest. Arlon moved at the wordless command, falling back onto the mat so Bridgette could straddle his hips. Her silver hair fell over her shoulder as she looked down at him, her face flushed with pleasure.

"Is this alright?" she asked.

Arlon grabbed her hips, a sound of need leaving his lips like a plea for mercy. "*Yes.*"

Bridgette hummed before she rocked her hips just so, and Arlon shuddered as his cock dragged across her entrance. His hands tightened on her hips, and Bridgette only teased him for a moment longer before she descended on him. The air left his lungs as her warm, wet heat enveloped him.

"Big boy, indeed," Bridgette said around a moan. She bit her lower lip as she settled fully onto him, her ass flush against his lap, knees resting on either side of his waist. He reached out almost reverently, his calloused hands stroking over her thighs, but he was distracted from the sight of her when Garrett came into his field of view.

Before Arlon had a chance to catch his breath, Garrett stole it all over again as he met Arlon's lips in a gentle kiss. The feel of his tusks added an extra level of sensation as the other man's tongue explored his mouth. Vaguely, Arlon realized he'd never been kissed by a man before, but he couldn't deny how it made his pulse surge even as Bridgette started to move.

Her hands planted against his chest as she rode him, and the sound of her pleasure was only second to the feel of her rocking down onto him. Arlon kept one hand on her hip even as his other reached up to cup Garrett's head. He deepened the kiss like he was starving, and Garrett groaned as he returned it in kind, tusks nipping and lips sucking.

Bridgette's moans were like music to his ears, and when Garrett finally pulled up for a breath, Arlon was able to see her flushed grin.

"*Fuck*, but that's a sight," she panted, hips never stilling.

"Could say the same about this," Garrett said before his hand cupped Arlon's chin, thumb hooking into the corner of his mouth. Arlon moaned as he sucked gently, tasting the salt of sweat on the other man's skin. Between the two of them, Arlon couldn't string a thought together, but it was a welcome sort of oblivion.

Arlon arched as Bridgette's pace sped up. He felt like he was going to come apart, shatter at last between them. "Not yet," Bridgette ordered, reading his body just as easily as Garrett did during a spar.

"Bri, *please*," Arlon begged, voice slurred around Garrett's thumb.

Bridgette slowed her hips as she smirked down at him. "I said, not yet."

Arlon swore as his hands tightened around Bridgette's waist. He held her still as he rolled his hips, trying to fuck up into her, desperately chasing his end.

Garrett chuckled as his thumb slid from Arlon's mouth only to grab his wrists. He pulled them from his wife's waist, his grip stern, before he pinned them on the mat beside Arlon's head. It made him feel trapped, but for once, Arlon welcomed the cage.

"Is this alright?" Garrett asked, voice husky with pleasure.

"Please, *please!*" Arlon gasped. He rolled his hips again, but Bridgette rode the wave of his movements easily, her slow, steady pace never faltering.

"You look so good when you're desperate," Bridgette said. Her grin was sharp as she leaned forward, grinding her clit against Arlon's pelvis as she said, "Almost, big boy. Hold out for me just a little longer."

"F-fuck!" Arlon shouted, his arms straining against Garrett's immovable hold. It was an order he didn't know if he could obey, but godsdamn, he was willing to try for her.

Bridgette's eyes closed, face scrunched as she upped her pace again. She rocked down against him, her back bowing as breathy sounds of pleasure broke from her lips. Arlon moved with her as best as he could until she doubled over with a shout of bliss.

"Let me see it, Arlon," she moaned as pleasure wracked through her body.

Arlon let out a shout of pure relief as his end crashed

through him. It felt so good it hurt, but he savored the ache that bloomed with every contraction. Above him, Bridgette's moan shuddered out of her as her walls rippled and squeezed in time with Arlon's own heartbeat. The pleasure seemed to last forever before it abated, leaving him breathless and panting on the mat.

He wasn't sure how long he floated in the haze of bliss, unable to string a single thought together. He just savored it, feeling safe and warm and satiated. Gentle lips and tusks brushed his forehead, easing him out of it.

"Are you alright?" Garrett asked.

Arlon blinked his eyes open and found the two of them looking back at him. Garrett sat on the mat beside him, wearing a smile that he just couldn't seem to get rid of. Bridgette had moved to rest her chin against the expanse of Arlon's chest as she grinned up at him.

Something in their attention cut through his haze of pleasure. Bliss turned to panic in between heartbeats as he came crashing back into himself. Every fear, every uncertainty flooded him, suddenly making it hard to breathe.

Bridgette saw it first, her smile fading as she sat up. "Arlon?"

"I have to..." he started, but he didn't know how to finish the sentence. His thoughts had ground to a halt, leaving him with nothing but the desire to flee.

"Hey, it's alright," Garrett said, but Arlon couldn't even begin to understand how.

He'd just taken a step he couldn't return from, and it felt like jumping into a pit without knowing how deep the bottom lay. Whether it would be a short or long drop before he inevitably shattered at the end of it. The thought of all the hurt that was bound to occur left him reeling, the fear squeezing tight around his lungs as he grabbed his discarded clothes, pulling his shorts back on.

"Arlon, talk to us," Garrett said, worry coloring his voice, but Arlon was already on his feet. He took the stairs out of the dungeon three at a time before he emerged into Fawn's office, but the Grandmaster wasn't behind her desk.

He couldn't stay here. Couldn't wait for Garrett and Bridgette to come up and prove his every fear right. He fled the office, but his room didn't feel safe either, not when it was so close to theirs.

Instead, Arlon went to the only truly safe place he knew and was grateful to find the door to Fawn's quarters unlocked.

12

"Arlon?"

He blinked aching red eyes, drawing his head up from where he'd buried it against his arms. He was sitting on the floor against Fawn's bed, but before he could get to his feet, Fawn sank down to join him. Her hand cupped his cheek, and even though he thought he'd privately shed every tear he had, she proved him wrong.

"Fuck," he muttered, scrubbing angrily at his cheeks.

"What's wrong, *a'marra*?"

"Did Garrett and Bridgette talk to you?" he asked, though he dreaded the answer.

"They did," she said. "They were looking for you everywhere."

Arlon swore, burying his face against his arms again. Fawn moved to sit beside him, pressing against his side. Her warmth was an unwelcome comfort.

"What happened?" she asked.

"You already know."

"I want to hear your experience."

Arlon swallowed the knot in his throat. "We had sex, and it was... intense, and I-I ran off. They both tried to ask me what was wrong, but I just... left them."

Fawn's arm wound around his to grab his hand. "Why?"

He kept his face buried against his arms as his tears spilled over anew. "Because I'm so fucking scared."

Fawn's long fingers landed gently against his back, and he couldn't help but flinch. "Scared of what?"

He couldn't stand her touch. Not now. He lurched to his feet. "Of losing you!" He swore and started to pace, fingers dragging roughly through his hair. "Of losing *them!*"

Fawn didn't miss the slip of his words, and all at once, she seemed to realize the reason he'd kept her at an arm's length recently. Her gown whispered as she got to her feet, coming to stand in his path.

"Arlon." Something in her tone stopped his pacing, but he couldn't bear to face her. "Look at me."

There was no command of hers he couldn't obey. He turned, his heart aching as he looked at her through tear-blurred eyes. She closed the distance between them before she took his hands.

"You know better than most that loss is a part of life, *a'marra*," Fawn said. "I'm a diviner, but I can't see all that the future holds. I can't tell you that we won't grow apart someday, even break off what we have. I can't swear that you will always have Garrett and Bridgette beside you. I can't promise that you will *get* a happily ever after. There are no guarantees with love, Arlon."

Arlon's eyes spilled over again. It was every fear, every doubt confirmed. He'd loved so few people in his life, and every last one of them, through death or betrayal, had left a wound in him. How could the Crux be any different? Fawn's mark was already visible in the scar across his chest.

"But that doesn't mean you shouldn't *try*." Fawn's hands tightened around his, and something in the touch helped ground him a little. "No matter what form love takes, it isn't a tree you plant and expect to prosper. It's a garden that has to be maintained, and you are only able to do so much of that labor. Some things are simply out of your control."

Fawn gave a small, humorless laugh. "*Everything* we do at the Crux is a risk. When we make friends, make love, make *magic*, we put our hearts on the line." Her hand reached up to cup his cheek, and it was only then he saw the unshed tears in her eyes. "What *you* have to decide is if that risk is worth the potential hurt."

Arlon's words died in his throat as he looked at her. He'd gotten used to seeing the woman behind the Grandmaster. But when he looked at her now, he saw someone who had suffered loss just as much as he had. For the first time, he could see her invisible scars like an echo of his own.

"Is it worth it?" he asked, his voice shaking.

Fawn's thumb stroked his cheek, but somehow, the tears lining her eyes only made her smile brighter. Like sunlight shining through storm clouds. "Only you can answer that for yourself, *a'marra*. But in my experience?" She gave a small laugh. "Yes. Always."

A rlon found Garrett and Bridgette later that night. When he knocked on the door to Bridgette's room, it swung open almost immediately. Garrett's expression changed from worry to relief to uncertainty in the blink of an eye.

"Arlon, I—"

Arlon shook his head. "No, let me talk first," he said, afraid he'd lose his nerve if he didn't.

Garrett looked no less uncertain, but he nodded before he stepped back to allow Arlon into the room. Bridgette was sitting on the bed, her hair still wet from the baths, but she offered Arlon a small smile as he entered. Garrett took a seat next to her, and Arlon noticed that it was bigger than the bed in his room. Made for two rather than one.

That realization burrowed into his mind, making him feel like an intruder as he pulled the chair from their desk and took a seat. He swore quietly as he dragged his fingers through his hair, his foot bouncing an anxious rhythm against the floor as he tried to find the words to start.

"I'm sorry for running off," he said at last. "That wasn't fair to either of you to leave you like that. Realization just... kind of hit me, and I panicked."

"Realization about what?" Bridgette asked, her voice gentle.

Arlon kept his eyes on the floor rather than looking at the two of them. He swallowed the lump in his throat before he said, "That I care about you two. A lot."

"If you're afraid the feeling isn't mutual, don't be," Garrett said before his lips quirked into a small grin. "We care about you, too."

Arlon shook his hanging head even as warmth filled him at the easy admission. "No, that's not it." He let out a long breath before saying, "I'm not used to... getting close to people. Getting close means getting hurt, and I'm..."

His voice trailed off, but on the bed, Bridgette shifted. Her soft footsteps crossed the short distance to the desk before she took a seat on its surface. She finished his thought for him. "You're afraid of getting hurt again."

He nodded, and Bridgette hummed before she rested an

arm over his shoulder, leaning close. "You know, when you picked that first fight with Garrett in the transmutation yard, I remember thinking you were either the bravest or stupidest person I'd ever met."

Garrett's chuckle rumbled from the bed, and Arlon couldn't help a short, surprised huff of a laugh. Bridgette grinned at him but continued, one finger toying with a strand of his hair. "Were you afraid then?"

"Terrified," Arlon admitted.

Garrett shifted off the bed and sank to crouch in front of Arlon, arms draped over his folded knees. "I knew I had rattled you. Didn't think I'd see you again, but then you found me the next day. Not just that, but you asked me to *teach* you."

Arlon frowned. "So?"

Something sad lurked in Garrett's wry smile. "So, running away is easy. Confronting the thing that made you do it is a lot harder, but you did it anyway. Now, you're doing it again."

Before he could form a response, Bridgette turned him to face her with a finger under his chin. "I'll tell you my biggest fears about all this if you tell me yours."

Arlon let out a shuddering breath, steeling himself before he nodded. Bridgette cupped his cheek, her smile faint and a little nervous.

"I've had a lot of lovers in my life, but until earlier today, Garrett's only ever been with me," she said, and Arlon straightened in surprise. "I'm afraid that as he starts branching out into the Crux, he'll realize marrying me was a mistake. That he rushed into it with me. That maybe he'd be happier being with someone else."

Garrett tsked before he reached out to grab Bridgette's free hand, squeezing gently.

Arlon looked between the two of them with wide eyes. "Am I the first man you've ever had sex with?"

Garrett nodded as he rubbed the back of his head, looking sheepish. "Was it alright?"

Arlon let out a small laugh, his shoulders relaxing a bit. "Better than I ever thought it could be. Still think I prefer being on top, though."

"I still haven't quite found where I fit in with casting and conduiting," Garrett admitted. "But, gods, there's a lot I want to try. I'm just new to... all of this, and I'm afraid I'm going to fuck it up. Fuck up my relationship with you and Bri by making some stupid mistake. When you left earlier, I was afraid I'd already done it."

Arlon swallowed as he looked between the two of them, finding familiarity in both of their fears. That fear of rejection, of making mistakes. The fear of getting hurt by someone you care about. He mustered his own courage before he said, "I'm afraid that if I get any closer to you two, o-or to Fawn, you'll all realize that I'm still the same person Vian made me. I'm afraid that if you know me, you won't want anything to do with me."

Garrett took his hand. "We already know you."

Bridgette pressed a gentle kiss to Arlon's temple. "We just want to know you this way, too."

Arlon looked between the two of them. That same pit he'd felt in the dungeon opened in front of him again, vast and unknown. Before, he had been convinced he would shatter at the bottom. Now, he was starting to think that maybe, just maybe, someone would be there to catch him.

"Yeah," he said on a shaky breath. "Yeah, I'd like that, too."

13

When Arlon entered Fawn's office two days later, she took one look at him before her face split into a smile.

"Those don't look like clothes for sparring practice," she said as she stood from behind her desk.

Heat creeped up his neck as he looked down at the outfit he'd picked out today. Clothes were his armor, and this outfit wasn't too far removed from what he normally wore—black trousers, a white linen shirt. The only real additions he'd made were the black leather harness that hugged his chest and black boots that reached halfway up his calf. He'd polished the leather of both to a shine.

"Do I look ridiculous?"

"No," Fawn chuckled as she stepped towards him, her fingers teasing lightly down his chest. "You look like a caster."

Arlon's lips quirked into a grin. "Is it alright if we use the dungeon today?"

"You've never needed to ask before," Fawn pointed out.

"That was when we were sparring, and today is... not that," Arlon said.

Fawn fixed the fold of the collar of his shirt. "Whenever the dungeon isn't in use, it's open to you. Whichever way you wish to use it."

Arlon took her hand before he pressed a kiss to her fingers. "Thank you."

"I take it that you talked through things with Garrett and Bridgette?"

"We did," Arlon said. "We've... talked a lot the past couple of days."

Fawn's smile only widened. "And do you feel good about those conversations?"

Arlon was fully aware that his blush had traveled to his face. He rubbed his cheek as if it would do anything to get rid of it. "I do."

"I'm glad," Fawn said. "Is there anything you need from me?"

Arlon looked at her in wonder, gratitude welling up inside of him like a fountain. He cupped her face before pulling her into a fierce kiss, trying to pour all of his appreciation into her through the simple contact of their lips. When he finally pulled away, Fawn's face was a little flushed, her eyes bright.

"What does *a'marra* mean?"

Fawn beamed at him before she pressed a gentle kiss to his lips. "It means 'my love'."

Emotion spread through him like a balm. He tried to think back when she first started calling him that, and realized it was months before he'd earned his freedom. Long before they'd been intimate.

She had known for so long, and maybe on some level, Arlon had known it, too. But now, for the first time, he wasn't afraid to say it.

"I love you, too, Fawn."

Fawn's smile lit up her face. As if she'd just been waiting

for him to say those words. She leaned up to kiss his lips one last time before she pulled something from her pocket and slipped it into his hand. Arlon looked down, and he couldn't help but laugh at the sight of the metal cock cage, wrapped with a key on a chain.

Fawn gave him a sultry wink. "Have fun, *a'marra*."

BONUS MAGIC

Want to see Arlon's first time casting with Garrett and
Bridgette?
Get the bonus scene "Caster" here!

ALSO BY ALETHEA FAUST

Main Series:

Initiation, Sex Wizards Book 1

Mastery, Sex Wizards Book 2

Championship, Sex Wizards Book 3

Odyssey, Sex Wizards Book 4

Side Stories:

Storm Night, A Sex Wizards Story

Divination Practice, A Sex Wizards Story

Starshine, A Straetham Story (Garrett and Bridgette's backstory)

Misfit, A Straetham Story (Arlon's beginnings at the Crux)

Coming Soon:

Homecoming, Sex Wizards Book 5

ABOUT THE AUTHOR

Alethea Faust is a writer of kinky, queer, erotic epic fantasy. Things you can expect to find in their works are risk aware consensual kink, hard BDSM, non-toxic masculinity, kind and emotionally mature adults, and so much butt stuff.

They also have a Patreon where you can find exclusive stories in the Sex Wizards world, as well as early access to future books in the series.

They can be found all across social media here: https://linktr. ee/aletheafaust